Brian Miller:
KATRINA
AND THE
STAR DRAGON

(A Zombie Adventure)

BOOK FOUR

J. MICHAEL BROWER

BRIAN MILLER: KATRINA AND THE STAR DRAGON (A ZOMBIE ADVENTURE) BOOK FOUR

iUniverse books may be ordered through booksellers or by contacting:

iUniverse
1663 Liberty Drive
Bloomington, IN 47403
www.iuniverse.com
844-349-9409

Author of Brian Miller & The Twins of Triton

With illustrations by:
Rachel Fort and William P. Brower

ISBN: 978-1-6632-2976-2 (sc)
ISBN: 978-1-6632-2977-9 (e)

Print information available on the last page.

iUniverse rev. date: 10/01/2021

A (VERY NECESSARY) INTRODUCTION

by J. Michael Brower

It doesn't matter *what's* said, only *who* says it!

The contacts made, the good feeling careered, reputations banked, the rank and position one actually has: That's the voice who is 'significant,' not <u>what</u> is actually said. But if you get nothing out of this 'reintroduction,' get this, which is important no matter **what position** you have:

An LNC is coming…and any fool can see that.

Oh, that's Limited Nuclear Conflict. I did have something to say, but this quote from Laertes (in <u>Hamlet</u>) I can't escape: "I have a speech of fire that fain would blaze, But that this folly doubts it." And just this about my writing 'folly': If no one wants to hear it, just write it! If it's not world-important, fucking keep it to yourself. But this is *world-important*. And an LNC won't be like a tsunami, or the long-overdue Cascadia Earthquake or a meteor (or two!), no, even global warming might be a little too late to start humanity's post-apocalyptic future. It will be like that battleship USS Maine blowing up in 1898, Pearl Harbor, 9/11—it will be a surprise, a shock, and so many Americans will die. Sure, the sun will blow up, or there might be a super flare someday. In 1918-1919 the flu killed 675,000 people in America; now it's 610,000 killed and counting by the COVID-19 plague...but nukes will take care of millions.

Pakistan, North Korea, Israel, the French, the British the Russians, us; an LNC is just around the Armageddon corner. Anyone reading Robert McNamara's In Retrospect or being a student of his, will know what I'm (dreadfully) talking about. Maybe some terrorist group will launch a 'dirty bomb,' in some kinda 007-kinda way: and it will make 9/11 an overture leading up to the main event—another kind of super-all-encompassing-war, that, unlike previously, the rich and the poor alike will be involved in. That's one of the reasons it hasn't happened yet. Recently, in I Alone Can Fix It, Joint Chiefs Chairman Mark A. Milley said, talking to House Speaker Nancy Pelosi, "There's not going to be an accidental firing of nuclear weapons." Wow, such a relief! Just another 'comical' mention: Saturday Night Live produced a piece on March 11, 2021, "A Geography of Who Hates Who" on the Daily Show. In sum, most hate us.

Yes, it's only a matter of time.

Maybe not tonight.

Maybe tomorrow night.

One night (or day, really, it doesn't matter)...**for sure**.

And it will probably be Unexpected, too (not like the cheese or dwarves visiting Bilbo Baggins), it will be dirty and short. But the effects of it, will last a lifetime. Nine countries, that we know of, have these weapons—and they never make mistakes, right? Nevertheless (and all-the-more) 'The People' can't fault themselves: All are patriotic, all want to do right, but all follow orders. Even in Oliver Cromwell's Protectorate, 1653-1659, he did 'God's work' and thought he was doing 'right.' Joan of Arc was a witch (1431), considered 'right,' at that time, then a Saint in 1920, considered right again. The Earth was flat (right) then it became round (right). Right? Was Stalin 'right'? Pol Pot? Trotsky? Lenin? Mao? Strange, the actual clothes, the apparel, wore by most human-averse dictators, is a uniform. They 'thought' they were right at that time that they were in power. With nukes, all of this is so, so avoidable! The people, even though well-trained, can't help but screw something up. Like my brother said about nuclear weapons, 'limited' wouldn't be 'limited.' Remember, Gene Hackman had 'checks and balances' on the *Alabama*, in <u>Crimson Tide</u>. In that fiction story, Denzel Washington won the day.

In the Cuban Missile Crisis, our non-fiction story, October 1962, Vasili Arkhipov, <u>disagreed</u> to launch a nuclear torpedo, saving the day (and maybe *this* day, too). Arkhipov was not praised when he got back home. Everyone says we were closer to nuclear war that anyone realizes in 1962.

Have we improved?

You can't impose democracy on native elements, I guess that lesson wasn't learned in Vietnam. Nature, in the form of DNA, is the watchword. All else is imperialism, is invaderism *writ large*. Can we trust the Indians, the Pakistanis and the North Koreans? And the Israelis? And the terrorists with 'nukes' in their pockets? Colin Powell was necessary in 1999 with the Pakistanis and the Indians to avoid a nuclear clash. There are over a hundred nukes in Israel, last I checked, maybe more than that. War doesn't like the 'rational' or the 'rationale,' however the more people you <u>have</u> over the button…losing limbs because of artillery strikes will be yesterday's news: Radiation will be the half-life, our forever-answer—and that's just the half of it. I have *that* described in one of my books, <u>A Dragon-Star Lives Forever (More)</u>, pg. 29-38, I better not repeat myself (ad nauseum).

On the fiction level (for now), one thing can prevent our LNC: Star dragons with their human teenage companions can 'swoop' down in the nick of time, preventing such a cataclysmic event. These are crafty teenagers, mind you, and picked (seemingly) at random. I'm not trying to be a Homer Lea (a story in itself!), but everything is money oriented, capitalism reigns, but there is another problem, being human 'n' all:

Love, sire!

…and, if there were to be an LNC, all the geniuses, the human minds, all destroyed in meaningless megatons. That's supposed to be a quote from <u>Amadeus</u>, and using it, really won't solve anything: it doesn't matter what's said—only who says it. Love is the strongest force known. Don't you <u>want</u> an adventurous fairy story where the good wins? If Kim Jong-un said it, if Vladimir Putin said it, then, 'love,' would have more meaning. Frankly, I think we in Oregon should feed the people in North Korea. It worked during the Cold War, wheat for peace, right? What if a nuclear authoritarian gets ill? It won't take long—minutes, really, what is the prediction of the Bulletin of Atomic Scientists today, 100 seconds or some such before Midnight? This isn't the first warning, but it could be the last. War (real war) wouldn't be like Gettysburg, lasting three days or more, but over and done in a meaningless whimper. The big bosses and the oligarchs don't say 'love,' at least not that much, and neither does our President. If they did, I could relax; that they don't, that's the reason your reading (or hearing) this now. But it's only coming from J. Michael Brower, consider the fool source, after all. As just a member of the public, you have to have hope. Nothing 'major' has happened, maybe nothing will?

Oh, and these nine books? What are they about?
Two teenagers getting with reluctant dragons to save the world.
If you can't say it in a sentence…revisit and revise the sentence and then you've got it!

On the subject of **war**, my analysis is definitely…deranged. I've been enlisted, a sergeant, a law enforcement officer, a military officer and my views are…unsound. One thing on 'police' I have to say: They see people every day and it's a bad day for the civilians involved. They are robots, I was one: I didn't speak out. I wrote. No one cared. But I had some peace in doing it, expressing myself in writing.

In Judgement at Nuremberg, Marlene Dietrich said about the Nazis, "Is that what you think we are? Do you think that we knew all those things? Do you think we wanted to murder women and children? Do you believe that? Do you?" Well, tell that to the six million Jews that died during the Holocaust. Every single human, all of them, must be immolated, utterly destroyed, and that's what 'real' war *really* is: **Terminator** them--everyone. And that's why it hasn't been declared, like the Constitution says, by Congress, since World War II. Like it says on that manuscript that Captain Willard took away from the 'terminated' Colonel Kurtz in Apocalypse Now: "Drop the Bomb exterminate them all."

All of them?

You can't superimpose democracy on any people that aren't wedded to it. It's in their DNA, and no 'education' is 'going' to bring out that higher culture. Twenty years in Afghanistan should have showed us that: like the British (1839-1842), like the Russians (1979-1989). Damn, we are dumb. They are tribal, nativist, religious—most officers know the reasons why—and they ignore it because they are wedded to The Military Industrial Complex. Thesis, antithesis and synthesis have no place with the fanatical (that is, 'fans,' right?). Their minds are closed, amen. They are all compromised. Eisenhower warned of this—ONLY AT THE END OF BEING PRESIDENT. Now, I've covered all this in the 'internal war' stuff in people's bodies, and that's the **ultimate-war**: The virus-women-children-men all must be destroyed internally every day in our bodies. Oh, there aren't women and children 'associated' with cancer, right? Well, I'll tell you what, **radiation**, enough of it, will see to all of that! As to 'outside' war: Military deaths are not for nothing: weakness breeds aggression and all humans have to end up like they did in Hiroshima and Nagasaki that we 'war' with—that's the real final result. Don't worry: Fukushima Daiichi and Chernobyl won't be enough—we have to go all the way, like good Americans do! We didn't do that in Vietnam: But...it was discussed. As far as nukes go, someone will fuck up. Iran, North Korea, Turkey (the defunct

Ottoman Empire wants nukes, but don't officially have them 'yet'), Pakistan, India, the more you have, the wider the margin that... someone will fuck up. See? My ideas are definitely 'unsound.' It's good that I'm retired from the military. After all, I was a member of GLCM (Ground Launched Cruise Missiles) in West Germany. And if you, the mass public don't want an LNC, maybe, just maybe, there won't be any. By the way, rich people, the 1%, can get radiation from nukes, too. People do, however, screw up.

Now, to do this kinda writing, I have to work. That's why I labor, get a W-2, and all. If I had a bunch of 'followers,' or 'prodigal saints,' I'd use them to finance this writing (and reflect their ideas), but alas! I just couldn't find the way and haven't hitherto. Maybe people don't like the way the dragon stars and the teenagers 'get along,' who knows?

As for writing, I've no idea what can 'animate' my scribbling today: Except for animation! Thing is, I don't know how thick to draw the legs of any stick figure. My deepest desire would be to have one of my books on Brian Miller animated; then, I could die a happy man. The geniuses out there will know a 'better way to frame it,' than I, a poor author, would: In a word, I'll be easy to work with!

Anyway, you have to have contacts. This-many-a-day, capitalism and consumerism and social media run, well, everything. No matter what you print, no matter what you say, it's all depended on the hierarchy of the social media, the "people on the hill" shitting down on 'yonder peasants,' it's all connections.

Any and every fool can see that.

But I still, still have hope: Maybe my star dragons can save us all. But, hey, that's just fiction (for now).

J. Michael Brower, August 2021

ACKNOWLEDGEMENT

For Rosemarie Skaine and Leah Brower

CHAPTER ZERO
A Plan(et) Ahead of Time

On the starship, Katrina sighed, wiped her brow with a smirk, smiling surreptitiously.

–Well…I *knew* what you meant.

At that, the Star Dragon whisked her lengthy sharp nails away at the Russian human's warning, quite unconcerned, as a good saurian ought to be. Her 'impregnability' was, again, getting the best of this supersized reptilian.

–What a Quisling, poppy-cocker's line of sniveling solid-white Albacore you're feeding me now, Katrina! And may I have another dish? Of tuna fish? Didn't you understand me at all?

The reptilian laughed, but then clawed and ripped into her command chair's armrest. The serpents incisors and canines, seven-inches-a-penny-piece, were quite scary to the uninitiated.

Katrina, however, *was* initiated.

And so, the Russian was relaxed, she was used to it. Whenever the Wysterian's native levity appeared, Katrina dashed out to meet it, sprinkling off her like an English rain, running with it, laughing back. Katrina beheld the creature and thought.

–Come on, I'm *just* saying traveling over time <u>and</u> distance, knowing that it's nothing for a star dragon such as *mighty* you, just *might* complicate things, your majesty. That is, your puissant-eminence, <u>complicate</u> things for me, not for you. Its better just to go to the Ocean World like Jing and Sheeta say, my noble and divine companion, to rescue Brian Miller and Littorian, the still-Lord of the Lizardanians. What do you think, my enormously, beatific but towering friend?

That, of course and quite obviously, is the way to talk to dragons, star dragons in particular. Praising there raw, unmitigated power, their courage, their level of sacrifice to others, all this and more factor into (any) conversation with them. Then, Katrina reflected on Jing and Sheeta, the new companions to the Crocodilians.

–That's the *Beach* World, not the *Ocean* World; let's get accurate, since we are dealing with distance, Katrina. Another matter: I will train you mentally, as we proceed, we don't have a chance for real physical training yet. I will be demanding on you, oh yes. Drinking my blood will get you prepared for our training later on...maybe we'll find such an occasion for physical training.

Action was terrifically everything for the Wysterian.

Etiquette is key for a human, especially for addressing a demi-god like the muscular Teresian. The reptilian stood just below 11 feet tall, sported seven inch teeth, twin fins running down to a sleek tail, and had an Olympian-plus (+!) body, and, for some reason, was 'showing herself out,' with a certain 'oiled' sleekness for her companion. Katrina wanted to see her as more than a Velociraptor on steroids, posed in a muscle-show. Magic, power and procreation were at saurian control. Everything of human-made 'wonder' was deemed somewhat 'superfluous,' with saurians around. At first it was hard, now it was easy to see her as a companion ought to see: She was Katrina's best friend, but they bordered on something more. The Wysterian, for her regale part, pretended not to notice showing off with certain intense-tenseness regarding her body. She had a tendency, Katrina noticed, to act like some kind of a queen, so Katrina treated her like Queen Elizabeth (the majestic) First.

Ostensibly, Teresian was into saving Brian Miller and Littorian, but, her latent attraction to her human companion was mounting. Teresian did not see Katrina as a loveable pet, the teenager commanded too much respect. The Wysterian thought there'd be a little time before arriving on the Beach World, hence her showing-out. Then the Wysterian directed the starship to Florida. They would leave the ship at the temporary camp in the Everglades. The guitars were calling to the Russian teen. They'd arrive at Dave's Guitar Shop in an extreme whirlwind.

KATRINA'S MUSIC

KATRINA EMERGED WITH A CHARACTERISTIC SMIRK (BRANDED OF the McKayla Maroney-kind), forcing her companion to snicker. The permanent saurian smile then grew appreciably. Katrina wanted to make the last-of-her-saurian-kind laugh. Yes, Katrina was versed in saurian behavior—she knew what to do. Teresian wanted things to instantly 'hurry up,' and she wouldn't be satisfied with anything less than this state of affairs.

The human companion knew that the Wysterian wanted action-_action_-ACTION. You can't win a war with words, you have to _fight_ it. Things taking time were not in this saurian's agenda at all. Quick action quickly arrived at.

—I hope Brian doesn't mind me taking $30,000 out of his 'kitty,' Teresa. You think he'll mind? I hope there isn't too much month left at the end of the money.

She had the currency in a small briefcase, bulging obscenely in the middle.

—Nah, I think he's got more extreme problems. After we get your musical instruments, we can help him.

Wanting to get started, Katrina, was instant.

–Dave's Guitar Shop has, in stock, all the electronic guitars I need.

–Let's scandalously *star-dragon-lee* go there! Address?

–It's at 1227 3rd Street, South, La Crosse, Wisconsin, my companion.

–And the zip code, my attractive human?

–You're saurianly kidding me, right?

–I am. Not about your being attractive, though. I don't need no zip-code twaddle, forget that GPS stuff.

So, in the time it's taken to read this sentence, the dragon-star cut a hurricane-wind-tunnel, down, down, and blew in the windows of Dave's Guitar Shop. They didn't burst, they just 'puffed' in. The dragon gamely came down with a big bolt of lightning and a roar of thunder that would put Thor to mumblin' shame. The clouds didn't support such a bellow, but she didn't want to 'come in' entirely unannounced.

The crowd of shoppers gawked, since it was a Sunday, it alerted them from their slack-jawed, wall-eyed look, Katrina hopped off the Wysterian, and put a hand on her bulging back.

–Wow, that was fun! You got here so fast! Luckily you had an 'atmosphere,' around me; otherwise my hair would have been blown back and straight out. I'd have look like the Bride of Frankenstein!

–Not a certain Wysterian's bride, huh? Don't be jelly now!

Teresian snickered. She was getting the hang of "jelly" for "jealous" just taking a joyous, and loose, ride on Universalian, the universal language. The human's Black World Sword sucked his teeth (at least that's the sound he made) thinking he could have supplied an atmosphere around the young Russian himself. Teresian just went on teasing. The Wysterian winked at Katrina.

–Sorry I deprived you of that hair-feature. A do over?

–No, thanks, my friend. Let's go inside before we get too many militant on-lookers. Speaking of people, incidentally, this is how they get to you, the on-lookers get to the families, see? They can look with disfavor on a person's family, maybe even kill them. That's how the mafia operates, the families become involved, that's just an element of human nature.

Teresian took a look around, at the many gawking shoppers.

–No, Kat. No saurian would ever go after your family. What an atrocious thing to do! You humans want to assign any 'aliens' you meet the things you guys 'like' to do. That's dead wrong. There are things we like, love and crave, but we, at least the dragons, aren't into getting all weirded out. We are above that kind of low-life thing, doing harm to families. Don't get me wrong, we believe in winning, that is, we want our draconian way. Families might provide 'guilt,' to you, sure, but no saurian would go after your family, as a foil to you. That's too easy. That's a fine example of anarchism, no authority at all, and that's something that distinguishes us from humanity. If we've a problem with you, we go after you. That should be more comforting. I will attempt to show you how to defend yourself against a dragon. Defeating them, we will see about that. I'd only interfere as my companion's heart ruptures under a dragon's teeth. That's not going to happen. Your worth it, that's how I figure it. No harm will come to you, as long as I'm around.

–Uh-huh, at least you're not being cryptic on me. What of Genotdelian's killing of the 30 companions? Weren't they sort-of family, my saurian queen?

–Not to Brian Miller. Besides, he didn't like their 'political orientation,' anyway. They weren't 'family' to him. What should I do for the present on-gawkers, Kat? Should I pose? Should I pose like the Incredible Hulk? What wimpy poses he has anyhow he wasn't athletic enough. And he, what, howls when he does that? I'd give him such a roar that would straighten his hair all out and then he'd be looking like the Bride of Frankenstein. No doubt! You see how I take your Universalian sincerely? I'm not copying you; I'm being inspired by you. Just give an alien some advice she can use.

David Parker had two early morning customers. He was frowning at his work.

Katrina was most polite.

–Can I speak to the manager, if you please?

Dave grunted, and didn't look up from his labor. He was busily cleaning the guitar strings to a Les Paul, the kind that Joan Jett may have approved of, and had his back to the door.

The star dragon and the Russian teenager just showed up 'automatically' outside the Guitar Shop. They swooped in on star dragon wings, so there was no Homeland Air Defense, no National Guard F-16s, no helicopters, no nothing providing a 'defense' against your miscellaneous dragon, just 'swooping' in. Teresian understood the radar that repelled on her frame, figured it out, had on her "Ghost Pro" as Brian Miller stated it, from the Black Ops world he lived in from time-to-time. No one noticed her until she emerged with her rapacious, toothy grin.

–Yeah, I'm that guy, can I help—holy chloroform rag!

Katrina then smirked.

–Holy cliché, isn't that copyrighted? Now, you're in trouble, Mr. David! Besides, this isn't Batman and the Boy Wonder; it's only a mere star dragon and a teenage girl!

Katrina put forth her seven requests, not concerned in the least with the surprised manager. David hadn't yet recovered from seeing Teresian. Still a little shaky and aware of Katrina's en-sudden 'requests,' David was at extreme labor, and managed to put forth seven guitars for his customer, with the Wysterian nodding her massive muzzle up and down, looking on approvingly.

These were placed on an elongated glass case. Lined up were a Peavey T-60, Ibanez Prestige, Fender Jaguar, Fender Stratocaster, double-necked Gibson EDS 1275, a Gibson Flying V, and a standard-issue Les Paul. On the opposite corner sat the mondo, black suitcase, the nuisance 100-dollar bills poking rudely out. Dave had his eye on these. With this one chance sale, he'd finish this building and so much more with the resultant profits. Katrina didn't care in the slightest and had, of course, no business sense at all. She didn't care anything about money or possessions. The star dragon could provide anything and everything, at just a whim from their companions.

Obviously, David was familiar with the recent advent of dragons, everyone had seen them on TV, YouTube, everywhere in media today, but he'd never met one. The saurians were struggling to leave the Earth. Teresian was the ultimate dragon, and David glanced up to her 11-foot stature of extreme muscularity, completely bagel-mouthed.

Just as Katrina was about to close the door, four gentlemen rumbled into the room, all unknowing about the dragon and teenager. The 'band' went right to the guitars to the left. Maybe, if they'd paid attention to the gathering—and curious—crowd outside Dave's Guitar Shop, they wouldn't have entered.

–Hey, it's here against this wall, this is a Fender Telecaster, and it sounds like—oh, my God, damn hommies, it's a dragon!

This stung Katrina.

–"Damn, comrades, it's a dragon!" And what about me, the companion to a star dragon, just standing here? Don't do a Frankie on us, your balloon knot be reinforced by singular human bravery. No squishes, hear? They didn't even notice me, Teresa, and this is the color of my solid depression.

–You're not as unique as me, sorry to say. Hey, next world, maybe, yes? Plus, and in added addition, I don't look exactly human, right, at least, *not anymore*!

Teresa remembered imitating Katrina, shape-shifting, for the Twins of Triton adventure, and then snickered. She fooled everyone then—well, almost everyone.

The leader of the band, Joe Michaelson just took advantage walking right up to the star dragon.

–Oh, glorious, mighty dragon star, we've a song to play for you. (Guys, geez, grab some instruments, get the 'guest band,' stuff, Dave doesn't mind, he's frozen behind the counter, don't ask him, just get it!). May we play it for you, most regale queen? Obviously, I know you're a female, and a most attractive one, too, I might add, your nobleness!

Titillated and much amused, Teresian just folded right in with the request.

–Yes, yes, please play for me. Katrina can join you, if she wishes it. Come on, my band, and entertain me.

The band had a song to sing to the Wysterian and they were aching to play. Katrina joined in on the musical rhyme, just picking it up, on background guitar. Joe began to do a solo, then the band started playing. Katrina was proud to play, and was using an Ibanez Prestige keeping perfect assonance.

> *Lonely, in the highest mountain,*
> *Covered with a winter satin sheet*
> *Will I find the great Wysterian*
> *Golden green in her sinuous design, muscles raging*
> *Can she, a star dragon, take me with her?*
> *A Companion to foil her lonely pain?*
>
> *I'm the one you want, I'm your fountain*
> *To fly, fly, fly high!*
> *God make me a hurricane to honor her*
> *To dance in her clawed hand*
> *Grant me the talking to you,*
> *A saurian of ancient wonder*

At this point the Wysterian started to dance, to the wonder of the band, the shop owner, and to Katrina. It was a dance of serpentine designs, almost a Shakti dance, with the curvaceous nature despite her gargantuan size. Dave's shop had vaulted ceilings, it had originally been built as a grocery store, which helped when she whirled and looped over and over with all the seductiveness of a cobra, the dance would have put all 'Shakiras' to crying shame.

The saurian was looking at Katrina when she undulated her hips with many fiery ab-pulses. The five-pointed scales were positively effulgent and fantastic, clicking her mammoth Wysterian nails together, like a drum, just keeping up with the beat of the song. The reptilian's muscular abdominal wall corseted and then grinded like chiseled, green rocks. This performance was just for Katrina.

The 'Shakira' dance was shockingly arousing for the band, and Dave shifted happily and uneasily, just looking at her.

And then, all the years accrue
Offering nothing unless you move
Fly us down to the beach, yeah
Reveling in your collage of knowing-ness, that's me
I'm nothing unless you're free

How could I not fall for you, my lovely star dragon?
Dancing before me, this is my passion
To appreciate you fully,
How can I ever be lonely, I can't be saddened
Not with those falcon talons waiving
How I'd love to be this kindly dragon's plaything

I'll live forever, discovering in my saurian everyday
The spray of the ocean on my face, so refreshing
I couldn't be happier, this, such a blessing
This time, this shouldn't be frittered away
Unless you're free
Everything and anything else, just hearsay

The song could have gone on, but the door clanged open, and two policemen came busting in. The band stopped, the tones ringing to silent silence.

–Everybody freeze!

As though *that* was necessary; Katrina just laughed.

11

–That's a perfect entrance. "Everybody freeze," what a lamentable and dorky thing to say!

Of a sudden, Katrina's Black sword snickered and did a slight advance towards the clean-shaven junior officer.

–Boo!

Without a word, the recruit just fired off his gun, all 15 rounds. The gun was aimed at Katrina's Black sword. The sword laughed at Katrina sarcastic comment, hence the officer aiming at him. The recruit saw it as 'aggressive,' so he fired everything at that laughing rapier. Katrina's Black Sword glanced and ricocheted all the bullets around the room. The sword spared all bodies, but not all objects from the impact. The bullets found guitars, the wall, and an occasional window, splintering and smashing the lot.

The band, Dave, Katrina and the hastily bored Wysterian were not hit. The facetious Black sword had an assessment.

–Now, now, my grisly officer. If you fire off that pee shooter again—

Katrina giggled, seeing an opportunity.

–What's holding you back, my sword? Why haven't you disarmed him? It's just because you're black, so limited opportunities?

The sword grizzled at that swattingly-egregious remark.

–I'll deal with you hereafter, you mischievous little human, I'll give you such an incredible spanking!

The 'junior,' put another magazine in, a flash-in-the-chamber-pan, while the two exchanged remarks. The Black Sword grew irritated.

–As I was saying, Junior Mint, if you fire again, you'd better fire all you've got, all 15 rounds. Then, we'll see what happens, and Boo, too!

The sergeant didn't have a chance to say anything before the firing began. It ended in about four seconds; the final shot deflected, going through the forehead of the recruit. The young man crashed to the floor, still holding the exhausted Glock.

–And I hit him all fifteen times, ever so slightly, and he didn't even feel it! The last shot entered his skull, brains blown out for your sickening pleasure, and now he's so grizzly dead! Congratulate me, my fellow Black weapons!

And they did, a Black Weapon fun-fest of laudatory things to say, all eloquently-complimentary.

Katrina gazed at the crimson covering the floor. The band, for their part, hadn't said a thing. They just stared donut-mouthed at all the carnage. Katrina sighed at the guilty sword, sarcasm-saturated.

–I guess you had no choice <u>but</u> to shoot him, right my Black Sword?

–Sure didn't, boy-howdy, he got so pwned didn't he Katrina? He won't be shudder-coining anymore, not to anyone!

The other weapons just chuckled and laughed at the weapons sure-reply. Katrina seethed, holding back a giggle, then lamented the case to her magical star dragon.

–I think we need your services, Teresa, so please you.

The Wysterian smirked, then came over to the spewn 'junior' mint. Her sizeable monster boots were caked in scarlet goo.

–Wow, yuck, a good working over did you give this recruit. He'll never look at law enforcement the same way again. This is my one fear, my band friends, the Black Swords. Even I fear them. I think they can be overcome by mental power, but that's another story. Katrina's sword could use some disciplining.

Teresian mentally took all the bullets out of the young officer, floated them over to the display glass, and deposited them there. Next, she took all the bullets embedded in the miscellaneous things around the room, making a grand total of 30 bullets piled in front of gawking Dave. All items bullet-smashed, magically mended. The sergeant helped the junior up and reprimanded him severely.

–Everything's to rights again. My children have seen the power of my magic to heal and make everything better. I appreciated the music, bravo!

The band inundated the Wysterian with smiles, and she toothily smiled back.

–Now, Katrina, attend! I'm growing rapidly and rabidly bored in this shop, tut-tut. Goodness let's go. Thank you, my instrumentalists, you were solid good!

Katrina chimed in.

–I'll just let you divide up what's there. I think the band should get 10,000 bucks, jes' sayin'. You cool with that?

Katrina favored her brand of English, adopting Brian Miller's to a Tee(totaler). She was done lugging this case around and just left it there.

–Oh, keep the suitcase, silly, boondoggley old thing.

Katrina's Black World weapons grappled and gripped all the guitars and a small box of picks. They bent their guards and hilts around the instruments, just so ready to leave.

Already, Teresian and Katrina got an aircraft carrier's supply of food and goods on the star craft. And almost that instantly, they were taking White Holes and Black Holes, attempting to get to the Beach World (as opposed to the "Ocean World," just accounting for Katrina's earlier mistake) without letting Time progress anywhere. Still, the journey would take them some hours.

–Yes, it would be good to go to this world and then go forward in time just enough—for your safety and comfort, my companion. I have decided this, and you're entirely welcome.

Katrina, knowing that the Wysterian wanted to make everything safe for her new companion, thought it would be a good idea just to go through <u>time</u> alone. For the <u>distance</u> that could be covered by a cousin of Tiperia. Her name, in the Brian Miller tradition, was 'Tip.' They seated themselves for a brief run of several hours, that's all the time it would take for the starship to arrive on the Beach World.

Katrina sat next to Teresian, innocently enough. Her angelic countenance successfully masked her coy glances at her companion's stunning enmuscled figure. The bulging cords in the Wysterian's pouting zaftig-chest, the sinuous arms, her powerful, long legs, it all made Katrina shake, but quiver with a pangs of desire, too. Then Katrina frowned, not recognizing these 'attractions' in herself, these unspeakable contradictions. They were quaveringly strange, but so arousing, too. The Wysterian displaying bonhomie and was smiling, was a woman, but an alien woman?

Katrina wasn't alarmed at the thought of just 'innocently,' playing around with her alien companion, that couldn't hurt anything. She just 'playfully' batted the notion around like a curious cat. In secret, the altitudinous muscles and ululating gorgeous obliques thrilled her to no end, and she wanted to paw the Wysterian with abandon but held back. She was curious about what Teresian 'felt like,' but a coy Mona Lisa smile was her mask. Could even a miscellaneous, gargantuan tractor make her stupendous obliques move at all? Katrina wanted to rub right then on her scales, just to see her fingers 'backed-up,' by the Wysterian's sinews. Were they, in addition to the reptilians stunning, bulbous abs, freezing, warm or hot? Katrina took count of the saurian's elongated, mega-structural-strengthened abdominals, and she counted 12 of them, just pouting out. Katrina would like to be sashayed right into those 'pouts' regaling that stunning saurian chest. They looked like bended steel plates, with an inch between them and Katrina knew she was looking at the finest set of abs in the Universe. In not-so-secret Teresian was flexing her enormous core in an extreme way, just to impress the teen Russian. And impressed Katrina was, just bagel-mouthed. Katrina fought back the myriad questions like a hero. The hero was steadily losing. She wished it would hurry up and lose terrifically.

As a newly-minted 'companion,' a concept still being Katrina-stamped, she reflected on things immediately past. Soreidian, intent to be the next Lord of the Lizardanians, had issue with saving Brian Miller and, ergo, saving humanity. Soreidian wanted no prolonged interference, indeed, an end to further companionship. Mankind should and could be avoided like typhus, cholera or an advanced state of tuberculosis. Littorian, for his part, tread on these ideas like a god. His stomping and talon-smacking all of Soreidian's concerns was irksome. In Soreidian's estimation, Littorian just didn't care. Brian Miller and 'his ilk' would take advantage of the current Lord of the Lizardanians.

To that, Littorian didn't mind at all. Littorian wanted the Companion Program to thrive. Soreidian was selfish—he and Danillia had companions, Rachel Dreadnought and Jason Shireman. For the rest of the saurians, Soreidian had no concern and neither did Danillia. The Crocodilians shattered that, in a big way, 30 dead companions the result. Peace was being talked but without Littorian there to see it done, Soreidian's hostility with Heritian during the Twins of Triton battle didn't spell peace—at least, not to the Crocodilians. Heritian died under the chomping bite of Soreidian, and there was human help, *Russian* help, besides.

Only Littorian could secure a time of bliss and renewal. Brian had rescued Littorian, but the attempt left him gravely wounded. Katrina felt Brian, through telepathy, and his life was faint within him, he was barely holding on. He cared about Littorian, well, just like a companion would. It went beyond family, and friends, no, it was more powerful than any of those things. She knew exactly what it was like; her attraction to Teresian was bounded by hoops of steel and titanium, unbreakable.

Katrina was desperate; and she would help the Lord of the Lizardanians. Soreidian must have almost killed Brian. She planned minutely, and nothing was left out. Go forward in time, and arriving, well, just in time! Then these two great companions would tilt the balance to favor Brian. In her arsenal was the Wysterian's power to heal and, goodness, it was Kat besides! Teresian could conquer Soreidian, if they had a sparring match; of this Katrina had no doubt. What could go wrong with such a flawless plan? *Everything.*

CHAPTER TWO

My Lost Angel

KATRINA AND TERESIAN TALKED TENDERLY, IN JUST *SOTTO VOCE*, AS 'Tip,' speeded them along to their destination, The Beach World.

–Tell me about the finite, one last time, now that you'll live forever, Katrina.

–Alright, my Wysterian. Since you'll never know it, Teresa, I'll accommodate you. You live time like it's your last day, well, *all the time!* You have tea with your friend and savor the sweetness of the sugar, knowing that the end will find you. The stories of the humans are legend and legion, and they end just so soon! You can 'die naturally,' or a disease or virus will get you. You see the setting of the sun, its rise on the 'morrow, and know that you can do nothing. I think that is where courage, bravery and all those things that can lead to the end of life, that's where they are, the human heedlessness of life, because life is so brief, and we know nothingness, beyond death, so well. See, we don't 'know' what this life really is, because we've been dead much, much longer than we've been alive! So all this 'bravery' is just poppycock, with the 'cock,' on the end of that noun, kinda like wormwood! We are fearless and have bravado because we don't understand life. Finally, this consciousness is ended—such is the life of the finite, and hope dies. Now the discoveries of *infinite life*, you'll soon teach me. Hope is life, and that's all it is, that's all in which I have faith.

The queen saurian said nothing, not even to correct her youthful conceptions of consciousness. The Wysterian assured herself that existence itself would teach her on its own.

Then, Katrina reflected on Brian Miller's marriage to both the reptilians, Clareina, Larascena, or Clare and Lara. There wasn't a stroke of misogamy in Katrina's thoughts, and she was intensely curious about Brian's arrangement with those saurians. The reptilian was nestling in semi-sleep. Stroking her hand over Teresian's puissant abs, feeling them dip up and down the alacritous bulwarks, naturally flexed, they were exceedingly strong under her touch, and Katrina had a bolt of understanding. Snuggling up to her mega-masseter muscle, causing the Wysterian to smile sleepily, Katrina knew exactly what Brian felt with the Warlord and the Lizardanian. Oh, yes, she knew. Katrina's DNA suggested to her that an entire, well-endowed saurian male village going at her could bring her all the incredible euphoria she so sorely needed. She was ashamed of this, but it couldn't be resisted. As she glowered down at the saurian's quiescent, resting countenance, any human companion would see her as beautiful and serene. Katrina kissed her just under the Wysterian's closed eye, eliciting a slight purr, increasing the permanent-smile.

She reflected on marrying. It occurred to Katrina that she could marry each race of saurians, a Crocodilian, a Lizardanian and an Alligatorian. Maybe she'd even marry Teresian! She'd have the same criteria with all of them, as Brian did, complete freedom, as anarchy dictated (or didn't dictate at all). Yes, just marry them all! The wantonness astonished her completely. She was actually considering, copulating with all three races simultaneously. Such ridiculous (and hot) thoughts crushed her firmly. She tried to control herself, but, just like it said in the Bible, in Genesis, chapter 6:2 and 6:4, she was under their spell, and *wanted* it, too. Katrina tried to shake off the biblical reference but looking at the nature of the many muscles saturating the males, the saurian males, she seductively licked her lips. She reproved herself horribly, but the same notion was there again, the mountainous bicep peeks as they posed before her, caused the young Russian teen to go all shaking and quivering. Like an unwanted dream, waking up and going right to the dream again, Katrina thought of Brian and Larascena. Now, with her star dragon here against her breast, she thought deeply of them. Of a sudden, she thought she heard, *All of Me,* by Don Felder, from the underground classic *Heavy Metal.* Is that what was going through Brian Miller's mind? All that and a galaxy-more: It left his drug addiction, to heroine, far, far behind in his cascading mind. Katrina understood how it was for a teenage boy, and she felt the same way, as a Russian teen, too. The star dragons now held their spirits, souls, and their essence, and they would *saurian-esque,* covet them deeply. If their saurians died, their companions would know death too, and _willingly_ so. Meaning, who'd _want_ to live after so much unmitigated pleasure if it couldn't be continued?

Goodness, no human companion that I know!

After sleeping three hours, the Wysterian awoke, but didn't rise from the wetted bed. Katrina touched her masseter muscle fondly.

–I'm not like you, my friend, but I can improve, if you'll have me.

–Oh, I had you, but good. Maybe next time, it will be better still.

–Something to improve upon, my Wysterian, for both of us. Maybe we'll practice yoga, get into some Sri B.K.S. Iyengar? Now, say 'Krishnamacharya,' please.

Teresian just waved her iron claws, smiling.

–Yoga? Maybe later. I'll get you back for that miscellaneous noun, so get ready and that in Universalian. Speaking of words, *Ready to go?*

At that, Katrina's sword poked up from the corner.

–Right! I'll make a shield around her. She'll be well protected.

Katrina was equal to the moment.

–As good as a star dragon's shield, do you think?

–Yes, "just so," to quote Larascena! I wonder what it's like to be married to Brian Miller, as Clareina and Larascena are!

Not a word on their previous liaison. Tip was sure it'd be followed by infinitely more. The Starseeker wasn't worried about 'such a thing,' going on in her 'internals,' she was proud that they were doing it at all.

Katrina looked out the window furtively.

–No Mickey Mouse here (not that there is anything wrong with that), my human companion, but let's get to it! As you know, Katrina, your rubbery body will know the full power of a Wysterian's blood soon enough. I hope you don't just transform into a reptilian. I don't mean you too, but I will be tickled to death if that is your fate. You will be stronger than Superwoman, I'll bleed that much for you anyway. I will give you a dose of my blood every month. In the meantime, I'll *kill* anyone getting in your way; you know I love you completely—and beyond completely. Who knows, maybe you'll be able to take on a saurian someday, I'm so taken with you!

–I'm taken with you, too, Teresa, and you're not just my arm candy, I'm so yours to use and use up! I'm extremely proud to be your companion, my vampire-ism be damned, too! I just hope I'll be, you know, accepted, in this feeling.

–Your accepted and <u>exceptional</u>, my companion. This mission shouldn't take too long. I mean, I shouldn't have to do too much. What can go wrong?

CHAPTER THREE

A Wysterian's Incredible Plan

—Here's the deal (and I make no apologies for being draconian when I'm instructing you), my delineation, so now I have your full attention. There now. Ahem, we can go anytime to the Beacher planet. It's better just to go there, quickly, since the Asians know the location. Then I'll only have to move from one time to a future point, and not worry about the distance. Of course, mind you, I can do it from anywhere, anytime I choose, but if this will set my companion's mind to rights, I'll do it this way. That's as much *paterfamilias* as this female Wysterian is likely to concede.

Teresian said it all as a "Wysterian Announcement," and Katrina struggled to disguise her snickering. Katrina was not for pushing the Wysterian and knew about the dangers of traveling over Time and Distance. As typical with any individual reptilian, she wanted action and that, yesterday! Katrina nodded.

—It's time, so to speak, my Wysterian. Inertia must rule over everything, just now, and propel us to our goal. Littorian and Brian are on the move. Soreidian's spell is on Littorian. Brian is coming to the planet, the Beach World. Brian's plan isn't complete (no surprise there, given his history).

–Yes, yes, that's where we come in—I can revive Littorian. My Wysterian magic over a silly Lizardanian spell at any time!

The Wysterian was somewhat 'hasty,' when it came to, well, anything. This was somewhat unlike most saurians that did have 'all day,' to do this and everything. Not so this saurian. Things that 'touched time,' got on the last nerve of Teresian.

The Wysterian starship was indeed superlative, but it couldn't match the Starfinder in terms of Time and Space. Distance did make some difference, to both the Starfinder and the Starseeker. In the end, a few weeks would pass on Lizardania, Alligatoria, Crocodilia, and Earth, but no more, that's all the Starseeker could manage. That was acceptable to the supposed rescuers. The result definitely was not.

CHAPTER FOUR
Time and Distance Know-How

KATRINA WAS INTENSELY CURIOUS ABOUT "TIP," AND WANTED TO question the Starseeker. Both of the creatures were 'women,' and Katrina was deep in thought on this point. Tip was the first-cousin to Tiperia, and wanted to 'keep up,' with her, and was only a step or two behind her. Tiperia was the *Starfinder*, Tip was the *Starseeker*. That was the division of labor. The 'Star-gods,' endorsed anarchy but, that being said (introducing a contradiction, now), the class assignment meant that Tiperia was the Master. Again, not God, but 'god' with a small 'g'—the dragon star knew that mistakes were possible.

Since she was young, Katrina cared not about the far-out or incredible things associated with the saurians, stating all her questions matter-of-factly.

—Now, Teresa, this ship isn't alive the same way that Tiperia is alive, right?

Although in flight, the ship wriggled around slightly.

—If you've a question, I prefer you address me, not the Wysterian, if you please.

—I'll just address you like I do with Tiperia, with pleasant respect, my noble starship?

—Oh, she is a fine choice for a companion, very good my Wysterian. I'm a cousin to Tiperia, and naming me "Tip," is convenient for everyone. Keep it all simple, as Brian Miller says. I wish Littorian would cure him of that nuisance stroke. Operating with half a brain around saurians I wouldn't recommend. Anyhow, Brian, given his history, is boarder line retarded anyway. "Brian," vs. "Brain," I see a little pun, and that's curiouser and curiouser!

Katrina just smiled at Tip's 'summary,' of Brian, said in a pleasant female voice. Katrina wouldn't relate it to the brooding and volatile teenager. That is, if she could see Brian again.

Sitting in the co-pilot's chair, Katrina just lightly pushed a button here, a switch there. The Wysterian didn't seem concerned at all, no matter how many things she turned on and off. Now, she smiled mischievously at the star dragon.

—Did I do something wrong?

Teresian just chortled.

Over the intercom, a voice, was gentle.

—That's why I didn't fire off any guns, dislodge our outer fin structure (no need for that), or engage our matter-anti-matter reactor to blow ourselves up. You'd better introduce Kat to some of my rudiments; otherwise, as they say, it's just curtains for us, right Teresian?

—I just thought it'd be fun to get you to introduce yourself a little further, just letting a banana-smoking-and-button-flopping simian push your buttons. Now grin. Let's see if you can.

—Oh, they are pushed. Good pun, there, Teresian. Not! A simian? Don't let her abuse you so, Kat!

Katrina was equal to the moment.

—I'm not a chimpanzee or an orangutan, you know, and I'm certainly not going to call a certain Wysterian a sorely worm or a surly maggot, either. I'm so above any Mr. Wacky-wacky and that hoaxer Mountebank that would hit me up to talk like that about our dragon-matron like that, there!

The Wysterian cringed a little, digging her ultra-nails into the chair's armrest.

–Uh, thanks, I needed that. Talk about awkward! You don't want me to bite you, next time we have a session, but I'll probably be rougher.

–Don't temp me, I'll take this vernal female reptilian on right now, if anyone's interested. Tip, you interested? Anyway, I'm glad of the female voice I'm hearing, that's pleasant, females rule.

Tip responded.

–Well, thank you, kind Katrina! Males play some part in it, though. But not much. Just look at the 'X' and 'Y' chromosomes for you humans. Their ain't 'much' on the 'Y' you know, jes look it up! The extent of the 'Y' is probably just 'sex,' *writ large*!

After a time, the Wysterian reflected on her ship, a well-known friend.

–I've known this starship for time-out-of-mind, (*your* mind, just as a for-instance). I appreciate, Tip, you're 'allowing' for my new-companion. Maybe you'll have to look away, my dear Tip, just next time, when I get Katrina in my chambers again. I'm going to make her a tiptop Raggedy-Ann in my claws; I'm so looking forward to it.

After orbiting the planet the entry door to 'Tip,' magically opened, by Teresian's force of will just to get thing started, and the starship dutifully yielded to the mighty Wysterian.

At that, Katrina was seized by the powerful talons of the star dragon and was gone from Tip's doorway. Tip then belched the whole crowd, Katrina, Teresian, and the many weapons out into the void. The sword had to maneuver around to find Katrina, but he maintained a protective shield over her. Katrina wasn't worried as she was thrust, rather forcefully, up and then landed, with some grace, between the fins of the reptilian, nestling between them, and then holding on. The fins, unsharpened, she held with both hands. All of it required, on the part of both companions, 'finesse,' but to the entire Universe, it looked like an 'effortless,' move.

Katrina glanced out with her invisible 'atmosphere,' protecting her, at the planet. She didn't want Soreidian's claws diving into Brian's flesh, and she shivered. With Littorian unconscious, and deeply within Soreidian's spell, her knuckles whitened as she held on firmly to the Wysterian's fin. She didn't see what else she could do but try to save them.

Katrina's star dragon blood was flowing through her, creating a higher power every moment. She had a long way to go, but to what end? Would she become saurian herself?

If that's my fate, it wouldn't be so bad.

She wondered at the saurian-Cyclopean back that held her up, tensing her legs slightly. Of a sudden, Katrina felt uneasy and somewhat venery.

Wow just look at the creature's shoulders, her trapezius, her dorsal fins, her incredible spine, all of it is entirely muscle throughout, what a strength she must have. Is this the beast I caused so much pleasure, before? I've got to feel this, I can see every muscle-cord in her, she's so strong, now why am I feeling so licentious and she's so—

Immediately Teresian noticed and took a look back with her large eyes, shaped like an upside-down pear.

—A problem with my back, Kat? That's new. You're touching it is arousing me. I wonder what you've got planned back there. I'm feeling vulnerable.

—Oh, it's a perfect back, so strong, warm, and exciting.

—Go on with 'exciting,' please, I'm dying to hear, just forget that other stuff. Talk on, Kat; go on with 'exciting'!

—That will have to wait for another session with you, my gracious Wysterian. I've seriously got to control myself, my precious queen. I just can't believe how, uh, excited I am over you (and through you). I'm somewhat (but not, I think, very) ashamed to grip you like this.

—Oh, don't be ashamed, no Katrina! I understand. Listen, it's because you're young, got your 'whole life before you,' okay? You can die by 'violence,' but I'm working on it! Just look at how extremely old I am, I'm just a regular cougar, right? The only reason people have a 'problem,' with your 'venery nature,' is because <u>they are old</u> and the memory fades in those humans. They should remember when they <u>were young</u>, and hot, like you! So is this cougar ashamed? Not *re-re*.

The saurian chuckled, and Katrina could feel the laugh under her legs.

They flew down, straightaway, to the beach, Teresian not caring for the resistance of atmosphere or space, to their destination. She resisted all, just like a good star dragon should. The Wysterian landed with a little well-meaning flourish, and then Katrina hopped off into the sand, looking at the waves.

The wings disappeared and the Wysterian did some stretches. And physical they were, too, just to show off the bulging muscles of the beast. She casually grasped her wrist and then made an indescribable upper-arm muscle. Even her biceps had biceps; the unconquerable muscle was over 50 inches, just over four feet. Again, the young Russian reminded herself that this saurian had the largest, thickest muscles ever. No one could beat her on the <u>power</u> incorporated into that wonderful body. Katrina tried to stay focused on the waves coming in, but furtively peered over to her companion. She never looked back, glued and fixed, her jaw dropping, appraising the sinuous design of her friend.

—Now, then (yeah, isn't that an oxymoron, a contradiction, right there? Universalian is just so funny!). I'm ready to go back in Time, weapons and Kat. Are you ready, my companion?

—Huh?

—Once again, we have to rescue Brian Miller and Littorian, remember? You've got to have your priorities straight. Down now, human girl.

At that, the Wysterian laughed hysterically and added:

–To coin Larascena, I can't take you anyhow!

–Thanks. Uh, that's '<u>anywhere</u>', my hansom saurian cougar.

Teresian just blew it all off, concentrating.

–This is the spot, on the beach, here. I think just six weeks have passed in all the worlds, Brian hasn't even arrived yet. Perfect timing! We are everything Brian needs now to keep Littorian Lord of the Lizardanians, and damn that Soreidian, he'll have to play second (sucking) fiddle.

Shaking off the mesmerizing-ness, Katrina reached instinctively for her *patent unctuousness*.

–With the Great Wysterian here, they are next to rescued already, my emboldened, strengthened queen!

A slight look of doubt appeared over the saurian's face.

CHAPTER FIVE

SAME WORLD, UNDEAD FUTURE

AFTER TIME TRAVEL, WHICH HAPPENED QUITE FAST, KATRINA estimated a few seconds, Teresian stomped her high boots, in total frustration. Teresian was cross that she, Katrina, and the Black weapons moved a total space of three miles.

She moved them in Time <u>and</u> Space.

She intended only to move them in Time. They were in a city, which wasn't there to start with, and it was cloudy—but not raining.

A large, dominating apartment building set the stage behind them, just on the outskirts of the metropolis. Another structure, only much taller, accompanied the scene, but it was just in its rudiments, but without the walls. Katrina could see through the unfinished building from where she was. She could also see the ocean and didn't think that much of their physical movement.

—We didn't move that far in, really! I can still see the waves. My supreme, mighty Wysterian, that's really the scavenged cat's pajamas, bravo!

The saurian was not interested in the obsequiousness that Katrina sent out, not just now. Teresian waved her seven-inch claws around.

–No, no, this isn't right! You Black swords, I'm holding you responsible for not correcting my calculations, that's what a student is for, correcting me when I go astray. What, you afraid of me? All of you, come back here, don't slouch away! I'm going to train you hard, harder, hardest, in my mind; my Time Travel class is calling you and all of you have a seat in it, including you, Kat! I could bite you in half, I'm so mad at you nuisance Black swords!

The Black rapiers were full of excuses, and the hatchets and knives gave way, happily avoiding the strictures of the Wysterian. They didn't want to feel her wrath.

–These excuses simply won't do. You'll have to do more homework here, in class, in my mind. I'll be, of course, merciless.

Katrina didn't see what all the fuss was about, and spied *people*, just sitting with their backs toward them, the wind blowing from the sea, and over their many heads.

–Teresian, my brilliant Wysterian, I've an idea.

The saurian, eyes wide. Katrina picked up a rock and then handed it to the Wysterian.

–Carbon dating, that's the thing. You see? You can tell by the radiation inside. Just use your magic, ahem. Then you can tell 'when' we are, your majesty!

The Wysterian growled since she was upset with herself.

–Carbon dating? My massive gods of Bling, is that all you've got to say? The only date I want is with you, my companion.

Then she smashed the rock into sand, with mincing force. Just as a-for-instance, she bulged out her biceps into Mt. Everest to impress Katrina.

–Judging from that rock-crushing, I can't accuse you of any kind of cellulite, not at all. Well, my Wysterian, I tried *carbon dating* and even that's getting *old*!

Teresian got a funny look, wincing up her muzzle. Katrina then swallowed.

–You'll never see me again, sorry to waste your time. Oh, you'll live forever, my dragon? I'm sorry to waste anyone else's time. Please pitifully laugh, okay? This joking shit, on which Brian is making so much book, is extremely exhausting and highly irritating. Teresian, my great and enstrengthened queen, here's another idea, just to lower your annoyance-level. I'll just go over to those folks, ask what year it is, and report back to you. So simple, as a certain Alligatorian Warlord is wont to say! They'll be able, with the bulk of them, to report <u>when</u> we are, to some degree, wouldn't that be helpful?

–Go ahead, I haven't recovered from your juvenile joke, so anything would help. I'm not done reprimanding my slacking swords yet. Now, see here, you two moochers, and listen when I'm telling you that—

While Teresian dressed down the swords, dusting off her hands from rock-sand, bellowing at the hapless rapiers, Katrina walked up to the sitting people.

The teen Russian was sensitive to the Star Dragon and didn't want to hurt her feelings. Katrina felt proud that they had achieved such closeness.

Katrina, just gamely, walked up to the 'sitters.' She approached from behind.

Meanwhile, the star dragon was looking at the sky, trying to figure out where she went wrong, releasing with dismay the Black swords from her reprimand.

Katrina didn't know why the 'whole population,' decided to 'sit it out' like this. Maybe it was lunchtime, she mused. As she approached, she saw that the sitters were on a long rail, next to a deserted roadway, internal to the metropolis.

–Uh, excuse me, my friend and I took a wrong turn at the corner in Time (just whoops!) and then we are here and—

The Black sword interrupted.

–Katrina, give them room, they don't look good.

–Look good, huh? You're imagining things.

Katrina just wanted to return with the information to help her companion. The wind was blowing from the sea, hefting over the heads in front of her. Now, with only 10 yards to go to reach the first of the "apparent" indolent loafers, she got a whiff of the populous. The stench hit her, almost *belting* her back. The plangent 'humanoids' were just this side of positively putrescent. The putrid decay and offal, the smell of feces and body-odor made her Lizardanian boots go all wobbly. She then struggled back, the plume of garbage, rotted flesh, the black-smell-of-blood, and all manner of near-human refuse smote her whole being. The smell penetrated her body and soul and did worse to the teen Russian's core.

Her sword, floating along with her, was instantly on alert. Katrina's sword, a female, had her 'spidey-sense'-going-wild. Most were in business clothes, but closer inspection showed them to be disheveled and unsightly. The humanoids had children with them, too. And they were chewing on them greedily, in this gloom-dimmed world. Katrina couldn't have imagined the fate of the youngsters, she was kinda concerned about herself, just now. The teen Russian's hand unconsciously went up to her throat, swallowing mightily. The sickness of the scene shocked her.

Fifty eyes peered up, black eyes. For those that had eyes at all. Some were completely blind. That was because of the mauling that they had, by their own people. You could see that right off. Some were chewing on their neighbors' parts, personifying the offal. Katrina knew a virus or plague was in full bloom here. The hunger in the Ebony Otherworlders was overriding. Their minds, icky, rancid craniums, registered hunger, and hunger infinitum. The blood was dark, black their eyes. They had to be infected with some mass disease, and all the urchins gazed desperately, longingly licking their un-lips.

The haunts stared at Katrina with a slack-jawed expression. Her sword, on cue, got between the girl and the animated forlornness.

The group rose as one person. They were lightening quick, but she had star dragon blood in her. She leapt back about 15 yards, so their teeth fell on nothing. The Black sword would have its turn. The female rapier swiped off the heads of the first of the fiends.

–Katrina, you spare some for me! You Black swords stand down, just let me at them!

Teresian said it all with humor. This new sight would get her mind off the error.

The dragon would live forever, had magic and was unlimitedly strong; nothing could hurt her (outside of the Black weapons). The Wysterian was already formulating plans for the Undead Super Un-normal. A malapert telephone pole came to mind immediately. It'd do for 'clearing a path,' the Horde crowded all streets leading to Katrina. That, thought the dragon, would never do.

The Wysterian leisurely strolled over to the sidewalk. The telephone pole was incased in cement flooring—just child's play. She uprooted it and went to work. She got around in front of Katrina and sent the less-than-unfortunates over any miscellaneous fence, swinging the telephone pole back and forth, lambasting and splattering the Undead against any and all buildings, just like a Louisville Dragon-Slugger. She doled out home-runs just as fast as they came in to meet the telephone pole, her salami tactics were awesome. The Wysterian's magic had the capacity to lift up all the incorporeal Un-beings, on this world, together with their nefarious vital organs, and tear/sheer them all. The chimera's made her labor quite bloody, too. All of the companions Black weapons were deployed now, floating along, taking the Undead at their throats that the reptilian missed.

Engaged with the eldritch 'Undead ebonies,' the star dragon was doing a 'time travel class,' with her <u>own ebonies</u>, the Black weapons.

At the same time, the colossal dragon was batting the Horde around with her telephone pole with disastrous results in her wake.

—Guess we missed out on the dooms-day message on this world, my human. Well, I'll just have to make up for it in the following way.

Just then, Katrina watched her companion bat-to-Undead-death all the fiendish within the Wysterian's proximity, pummeled them into the wetted ground. Teresian was having a good old time, Undead-man-spreading them all, considering all her 'victims,' happened to be (un)dead anyway. A couple of them got through. Teresian put the telephone pole down for a split second to have her way with 'these lucky few.' The Wysterian lifted them up by the legs and then ripped and split them out in front of her. Then she cast the half parts into the Horde with an extreme laugh.

Of a giantess-sudden, shells came from the apartment building. A series of explosions pounded within the piss-pot corpses, just out of range of the companions. Then, a machine gun sounded and the front line of the animated horde suddenly developed holes in their frames and heads. A second semi-automatic was at work, too. Those with a head-shot just fell over dead, but the others just came on, only a little slowed-down, missing some of their appendages.

Of the Unbeacherly Undead, they were superhumanly (or super-Beacherly) strong. All were skinny, but that masked a body that was lithe and had a preternatural strength that was just astounding, and, above all, they were Jackie Robinson-fast.

The onslaught was felt on the carnivorous Horde. The resulting pile of bodies stacked up the streets, and a traffic jam of cadavers developed quickly. The apartment building was the center of the attack. The dragon knocking around the odd-hominids caused a pile-up against two buildings. The (vast) rest couldn't get through.

The girl operating the mortar Katrina could barely see. She admired the Asian and Katrina was amazed that a planet at the far-end of the galaxy had humanoids looking, well, human! She was busily putting shells in at a rate of 20 per minute and making adjustments via her partner's instructions.

The swiftness, at which the Undead ran, almost *galloped* along, amazed and flummoxed the Black weapons. Whining like banshees, those suffering (if they <u>can</u> suffer) decomposition were fast. The levels of peremptory-and-post-putrefaction didn't encumber their rapid pace. They charged at once, pell-mell, and the hatchets and the swords were forced back. The knives were the 'redoubt,' just preparing for a last stand. The Black weapons got their share in of the mundane people; heads were rolling crazily around like an apocalyptic bowling alley. The swords were frustrated, and then began taking the living dead at the midriff. They didn't care about the 'bowling ball' head-shots that the hatchets seemed to want. None could get to the mysterious, brutish dybbuk directing them. He was too well protected, the un-dead, being replaced by 10, 100, 1,000 festering faces, too much to chop threw. The Black weapons had never seen such a willingness to die (all over again), ever. The black blood was everywhere, universal, even the air was rent with the splattered dark filth.

The rampant, edacious Undeads weren't even humans; they just looked a little human-esque. So beating them around was not a problem for the enstrengthened Wysterian. In fact, Teresian was really enjoying it.

The reptilian, a little way behind Katrina, was shocked and partially tickled to see so many 'potentials' offending her companion. The danger such little Undead creatures could do was minimal, according to 'star dragon policy'.

–Teresa!

The consternation was getting to the human companion.

–What's concerning you now, my amicable Russian, isn't this fun? I'm just having a good time with these frickin' ghouls don't stop me, my human!

–Happy you're enjoying yourself, but we've got other things to do, my saurian eminence. Let's just see our 'saviors,' giving these fiends a little break, right?

–Oh, very well, very well. Honestly, Kat, I'm getting a little sick of your incessant pedantry!

Then she mowed down all the spectral supernaturals approaching, just as a happenstance, sending her telephone pole barreling into the impish trolls. The move was done in a 360-degree arc, mowing them all down, or knocking them backward, a funfest of meaty, destructive-esque-guts.

The weapons did the work of butchering the Ebony Other-wonders. As they did that, the impromptu 'Black World Safety Line,' was drawing slowly back, angling the companions to the apartment structure. The Black Swords were amazed at the willingness of the supernatural-soulless to come forward, even with so much death about them. Of course, they were dead themselves, so their losses didn't impede the orders of 'attack' given by their commander.

Katrina then shooed the star dragon into the structure's vast waiting room. Outside the apartment was a steel structure, way passed its day, with Armageddon in full spring. Quick as a graveyard wink, Katrina piled up the beams outside the residence, making a mighty barrier, and then got inside herself.

–Young Russian! Are you trying to make me angry? I was just getting into it, and you've delayed me with shoving me into this flat-of-Beachers! This isn't the 'unchained' Katrina that I knew. You other teens are to blame, too! What excuses do you have? I am so waiting!

The star dragon was laughing at it all, but no one else was. Nausicaa spoke up.

–Moving that art structure outside the apartment building was just awesome!

Katrina's pride just sprung like an under-used muscle.

–It was nothing, nothing, but thanks. I have to calm my star dragon down, you (should rightly) understand.

David Williams and Zhao Ziyi just glowered gawkingly on. Zhao was completely taken with the dragon, and seemed not to notice Katrina's 'almightiness,' at all. Dragons for her, well, it was like seeing a ministering angel. David thought they were both powerful, so plucked up all the 'niceties' he had, just then. The 'plucking up,' wouldn't last that long.

–It's good that you're speaking Universalian. Now we'll all know something. I didn't mean to interrupt the Beacher notice of my mighty star dragon fighting those zombies, please forgive.

David was perplexed.

–Huh? A Beacher? Didja' hear that? What's a Beacher?

–It's better than calling you an Earther, but it has the same number of letters in it, just like Brian Miller and Harry Potter have the same number of letters, jes' sayin,' my Beacher, capisce?

–Miss Dragon, your side-kick is strong and, er, just a little crazy, too. Not trying to offend you, but _damn_.

–Katrina's my side-kick? That is so fetch! I know you _want_ to like her, but you see problems, my teen Beachers. I understand. If you knew her as I do, I'd just have to kill you. You understand.

The Beachers were stunned.

Teresian laughed uproariously at her (most) private joke.

The Asian-looking girls just smiled at the two new visitors and didn't act afraid. Like all Asians on Earth, so far away, both teen girls were attracted to the star dragon. Katrina thought that was a good sign.

–And thanks for saving us with that mortar and machine gun, (I guess). May I introduce to you a star dragon, Teresian, my new-found friends? I had to interrupt her from having a good time with your resident de-gravers; she'd likely have destroyed the whole bunch of them, she's so godlike. She's a Wysterian, a dragon-star, (too much awesome class for a silly old demon) and awesome-strength is so inadequate to get a measure of her ultra-power-spectacular. She likes riddles (well told), is curious, and finds power to be her BFF.

I'm second-best BFF, and her companion, and honored to be so. We've got a mission to perform, too. I'm sorry to deprive you, my Wysterian, of playing with the Undead. If you want, my noble lady, I can send—

Teresian chimed in, growing impatient because the introduction didn't give her a chance to talk (well, duh).

–And this is my teenager, my *bootiful* and brilliant little Russian, before you now. She's got awesome Wysterian blood in her and would put Superwoman to shame. Katrina is a natural leader, an astounding blonde-haired-sinuous-and-short-tempered beauty, if you make the mistake of <u>rattling</u> her (I'm not talking about <u>snakes</u> here, not that there is anything wrong with that), and we haven't got all day to tell you of her awesome-ness. That steel arrangement outside this tenement made out of that ornamental thing was just a small sample of her mega-almightiness. Oh, by the way, the Black weapons, quite talkative if you give them the chance, have green guards for males, cherry for females. I'd get to know them personally for your safety. Of Katrina, she's notably honorificabilitudinitatibus, so giving her just awards is highly desirable, my Beachers! And I'm not being a 'flapdragon,' to say that, so there! Explain that Kat! Look at this, I just blew Universalian away! Zeus is just my errand-boy, let the pigeons loose and looser(er)! Just taaaaa-daaaaa!

The Wysterian felt absolutely proud of herself. It is rare to go on about someone else's power, as she had done, all in a flourish. Katrina was stunned, too, but let forth a civil response.

–Thank you, my lady, for so fine an introduction!

–You're quite welcome, my companion. That intro I gave you was just unprecedented!

Nausicaa Lee and Zhao Ziyi regarded the theophany-filled and pulsing dragon, particularly her corded physique and so wanted to shiko right at this first meeting. They resisted the urge to genuflect, with an extreme effort. The dragon had as much 'regalness,' here as they did with the Asians in far-away Earth. They snapped out of it, the fright overruled the majesty of childhood days were dragons walked (or flew). They smiled but had an eye towards the door. They were worried about the steel girders.

Zhao Ziyi plucked up courage overcoming her timidity.

–This is Nausicaa Lee and she—

Katrina's eyes got bigger and a smile appeared.

Zhao stopped, questioning.

Recognizing the signs, Nausicaa waved a hand, tediously, as though she'd explained this thousands of times.

–I was named because my parents had an appreciation for the animated films of Hayao Miyazaki. Still, I'm not ashamed, and I sure liked all his anime, and—

–It's amazing that on this planet, all that distance from Earth, that you'd know about Japanese anime, and have the same names as Earth, and even know of Hayao Miyazaki, it's just incredible and bewildering.

Nausicaa grew impatient with Katrina's speculations. Zhao just took over.

–I'm Zhao Ziyi and we're going to get Robert Fisher. Bob is great at logistics, getting everything the group needs, well, when we had a group. Bob is real good with—

David interrupted.

–I'm sorry, little missy, but that won't hold them, just talking about your shitty barrier show.

Both Nausicaa and Zhao jumped back at the comment. Katrina stopped abruptly. Katrina pawed the ground with her Lizardanian boot, snarling, and found herself listening to the teen male, the guy with the heavy machine gun. She found the flourish of mutual introductions struck a dull cord with him in particular.

Teresian, as was her wont, spoke out.

–Tell them what you want, intros are quite over.

Katrina knitted her brows and spoke forcefully.

–You Beachers come with us or die. You are?

–Shit, David Williams and I'm the leader of this group (what's left of it), and this is Zhao Ziyi. Robert Fisher is on the fifth floor, getting guns in the manager's office. Zhao is military-trained and is good with mortars and I trained her. You see, we came from a larger group, now decimated by that virus ridden—

–Yeah, can-it, Mr. Shit David, I've no time for your obvious twaddle, no time to yell at your fat, funky, fool face.

It was clear they hadn't the necessary protocol to 'doff the hat' and praise the star dragon, which should have been their first words, at least in Katrina's estimation.

Simultaneously waiving her hand and entangled blond head around, Katrina had an announcement.

–The star dragon and our Black weapons are going up to the top of this apartment building and flying off to the beach. Any zombies we see we'll consign to shish kebab. We went forward in Time too much. Details when I give a shit. Personally, I'm for making a hole right in the side of this puny structure and fly there straight-a-way. But first, we'll get your friend on the fifth floor. Y'all want to go to our world, you can, this one is two doors from hell. There's a stairway, we'll just take that to the—.

David interrupted Katrina, seizing her sinewy arm.

–I wasn't done talking, sweetheart.

Katrina goggled down and posed a question.

–You seemed done. Now, you want to lose that appendage? You are one shallow piece of shit. I'll rip it out of your socket, hear, Shit David? I should have foreseen that you were the worst of my 'David' collection.

David gingerly took his hand away.

–Listen here you some kinda scary tom-boy, we've got a guy on the fifth floor getting guns, and—

The Wysterian added in, quite unannounced.

–Good, then. We'll get him on the way up. Remember, one's lamentation is just another person's self-defense, okay? After we get this other Beacher, we'll just have Kat make a whole in the wall, or I will, then I'll take all the teens and up we'll go, deeds not words, my children. It's just so simple!

At the 'my children' comment, the Asians mysteriously moved closer to the Wysterian.

Just like that, negotiations were so done.

–Follow me—my children!

The Wysterian could no longer be seen by the teens, she was making her way up the stairs, in a snake-like pattern. The teens attended the steel girders and they were _moving_. The horde was hard at work. Katrina was shocked; the Still-Loosely-Membered must have been super-strong to do this or their numbers where great indeed…or both.

David explained that they were once part of an 'immune-train,' a group of natives that were _virus-less_, they had one guy in charge. Now, this same guy, felled by a zombie, was gunning for all four of them. This leader of the Undentables had no name, but the four teens called him the 'Intelligent Zombie' and he was ex-military. Since he was their old leader, the teens feared him most.

Between the girders so recently laid by Katrina, she got her eye on the Intelligent Zombie, just by chance. The 'IZ,' on a little hillock of bricks and broken glass, watched the young Russian's progress with a sinister brooding. The IZ was just under 10 feet tall, looked like two gorilla stuck together, with, appropriately, a goo-spooked-demeanor, with hands that could cover (but not crush) the Wysterian's. His chest was broad as any given double-door, and his over-all structure rivaled a full-grown saurian (minus that nuisance tail, scales, superfluous fins—the point is, he was Atlantean). He had the standard, rancid doll's eyes, mauled face, slack jaw, and the smartness and craftiness of a Cro-Magnon man.

He eyed Katrina up and down, as far as he was able, through the thin slit in her impromptu defense construction. This girl wasn't just a 'mere girl' she was superhuman. Then he spit hard. He didn't wonder at 'why,' a limit to what brain there was. No, these were the facts. The mortar shells and machine gun fire coming from the apartment didn't impress him much. They fell on his horde, and many were lost, but he had plenty of them, literally millions. All over the world, his 'request,' went into the minds of the so-Undead. They responded, all coming to the stricken city-by-the-sea. They were hungry. And there was superb food there.

The Leader of the Rejects of Hell could think intertemporally, at least at its rudiments. The IZ knew what was past (recalling the time he was hungry), thought about the present (he was hungry now) and could think about the future (he'd be ravenous again). Also, he didn't care who was under his booted, iron heel. Katrina could see he was dressed in raggedy military clothes. She knew this was the Undevil's leader.

Katrina's right hand rose to her green eyes, poking up to her own orbs, and then at his black eyes, pounding a fist together thereafter. This made the IZ sneer. The satanic Undead leader stopped and did the same action right at Katrina, the 50 yards between them no barrier.

> *All of this, between me and you, girl.*
> *Yes, between us, no one else—I'm looking forward to this!*
> *You'll become as We.*

Katrina couldn't be sure her telepathy was working on the IZ. He then smiled, revealing his fang-like teeth. Yes, her telepathy was working fine, too well, actually. Katrina did her characteristic MaKayla Maroney smirk then turned to chase after the star dragon and the Beacher teens.

All the Wysterian's weapons followed her, save the knives, which were watching the younger still-people. All the other Black weapons were bloodied to the hilt, and the blood didn't 'wash off,' when they stroked and whisked themselves downward at the ground. This was the most frustrating thing about the whole enterprise, too, the black, caked blood on their erstwhile ebony sheens.

Oh, you're black already, what's the problem, your frittering so much! You're going to drive a certain saurian crazy with your mental kvetching.

My esteemed lady! We can't wash this stuff off, the choppers' blood; we've never seen anything like it!

Isn't this what you wanted, adventure?

This is the wimp answer, and, yes, I'll give it: Not like this!

You want to just fly off this planet, run away, you can, you know, my good sword.

I wish to stay with you, and the Beachers and our human. As you know, I'm in love with Kat's sword, too. Can you have me in spite of my wimp attitude?

You're my A+ student in my Time Travel Class. Kat is just auditing, there's the wimp for you, ha! I'd have to fail her, she just can't keep up. This class is almost complete. Sure, I'll have you around, all of you weapons.

Thank you, my Wysterian.

They stopped the mental talk, and the sword jumped.

—Hey! Where are Katrina and the Beachers?

The teens raced along the stairway, trying to overtake the saurian. Almost at the third floor, Katrina, leading now, came to a stop.

—Please wait, Beachers. It's better to lose a few minutes of this life, than life in a few minutes.

David, his 'nice-ness' all gone hit back.

—Again, crazy as shit with your gawd-damn flim-flam. God, isn't she 'the One'? What an annoying little *she-ape* she's just like a frickin' clown.

Katrina bristled, her muscles involuntarily pulsed.

—I look like a clown to you, Shit David?

David hesitated briefly.

—Well, you've got to have some reason for your foolin' about.

—I guess haters gotta hate, huh? The dumbassery is strong with you, Shit David. I'm for arming you different. All of you Beachers will need a knife, from the Black World. Now look, they can talk, can float around cutting heads off, you bet'cha, now these are for you! I'm warning you; don't be separated from them for any reason, alright?

The knives attempted to get 'attached,' to each of the three Beachers. However, the knife assigned to David was refused with some fanfare. David was flippant and, hand raised, he backed away and had the following assessment.

—I ain't you're step-and-fetch-it, screw you, butter-knife! My .45s are better than this ole plastic piece of shit. I'm not having that nigg-nogg attached to me, no-Tom-Boy. And you've got a cherry 'fetch' to you? So you're a girl, is that it? This is a bitch-and-a-half, maybe even two bitches! What a mother ball-sack you are, cum-laude-blackie-pants.

The knife was just as shocked as seeing the Lovecraftian god 'Cthulhu,' come crashing through the wallboard with his hideous tentacle-head and sub-elementary wings. The knife <u>did</u> recover with some grace and acid-biting voice.

—I'd slap the taste, teeth and tonsils out of this motherfucker's mouth, but I'm on my good behavior. You stupid shitbag, you've got good-sense cancer, you suck a bag of massive dicks, fricking sloth!

The knife took up a guarding position next to Katrina, 'floating' on her hip. He rubbed on her leg, agitated.

—And don't assign me to a bagel mouth shit-bag like that again, human! Don't fool yourself, your no woman rainmaker. This whole thing about being a hopeless 'yandere girl' is rickety-lame. I'm just resisting giving you an incredible knife-spanking.

Katrina was surprised.

—Let's go, and at a definite run, too.

At David's refusal, Zhao Ziyi held up her hand, refusing a Black knife, too. David was her leader and she blindly trusted him. The knife sulked back to Katrina.

Nausicaa, on the extreme other (other!) hand, felt graced by her knife, one of Teresian's and welcomed it. She decided to address the knife, as they jogged along the dimly lit corridors.

–Do you have a name, my friend?

–That you call me 'friend,' is a good first step. I'm a female, hence my cherry color. The males have a green tinge on their hilts, shoulder and guard, you can see it if you look closely. I don't have a 'name,' but if some astral Undead appears, you'll know what to do with me. I sorta like to be thrown, you know. This increases the thrill, you understand.

Nausicaa swallowed.

–I think I'd prefer you in this fight, and just prepare to be thrown.

Katrina recognized the *click-click-click* of the Wysterian's talons on the tile, above. Zhao left her mortar behind her; it was almost out of shells anyway. She was armed with two Uzis and two hand guns, .357 models. She secretly regretted refusing the Black knife, following David blindly.

David Williams had .45 pistols, four of them, and his pockets jammed with rounds. He didn't feel he had enough, no one did, guns and ammo wouldn't hold back The Sorrowlers. The Beachers left a sting in them, but it was only the Black World weapons that posed a match to them. As it stood now, the Undead were pouring into the city, every floor beneath the group filled in with the revenant, angry for blood-still-not-spilled. Yes, the Beachers and the two companions could shatter the first and second lines of the Undead, but what of the third, fourth and fifth columns? The shambolic nature of the fiends was transforming into an organized massive Un-mass. Still, the teens had no time to talk, though they wanted to find out about each other, they just followed Katrina right along, briskly. Any talking they did was between jogs, running the stairs, up the building. The Horde filled up the floors they left like a tsunami, they were that close behind them. All the fire-doors shut and locked by the Beachers, up the stairways, the besiegers split open, pouring through.

David, just like the IZ, was indeed shocked that this 'mere girl,' could lift thousands of pounds just because of star dragon blood. The companionship could lead to unmitigated power, which really drew him.

David wasn't thinking about the future. It served him well, post-Armageddon. In the 'before life,' he was nothing, was considered border-line-half-a-'tard, by cruel adults. However, he showed all of them—dead and Undead alike. He grinned with panache, looking at the Horde roaming the streets. He was King of the Group, maybe the last group of humanoids (or "Beacheroids" according to Katrina) on the planet. Companionship, with the star dragon blood granting him unlimited power, attracted him. Since it was offered, even David Williams wanted to go with the star dragon and her erstwhile human. He was having a hard time with the two companions, and he showed it, anon.

For their part, this was a trial by fire for the hatchets and the knives. They'd never been off the Black World before and had no experience other than the willingness to go with the saurians and the human companions, for "the adventure," it promised. Even the two swords were at a loss to understand the Beacher Horde upon them. The IZ controlled it all, watch the Black World weapons intently, and had a strategy all prepared. The hatchets, knives, and swords could not understand it. The phantasms did not let them float away, and thereby strike at their necks at light speed, but actually piled on them. The weapons got bloodied early and they could cut through the numerous haunts, helping with any fight. But it took time to slash through the Horde, and in that time, more of the devilish could bite the star dragon or Katrina. That'd be all that was necessary, because the Black weapons answered to the two strangers. Once they were 'controlled,' the weapons could be ordered away by a soulless Katrina or the star dragon. That was the Intelligent Zombie's strategy.

The IZ raised his hands into the air, and his many lieutenants, nodding obediently, hurried to the Horde. They started a pile-up, all of them crushing into the building's first floor, just on the outside of the structure. The pile-up grew and grew, 10,000 ferals, 20,000, 50,000, more and more. Then the IZ walked up the corpses to the fifth floor, literally stepping on their vacant faces, shoulders, hands, backs, up and up. His miniony lieutenants followed, about twenty of them, the raggedy remains of a once proud people. They were hungry for Beacher flesh, and the two new creatures, too. They didn't understand much. But they knew how to follow orders from the clever, monster cretin that could feed them.

The itinerate entities all piled on to one another at the left section of the apartment building. The IZ and his lieutenants directed them. They dutifully followed and would till the un-dead end of them. On and on they stacked, faces twisted. They formed a triangle on the left side, up to the fifth-floor windows, amassed.

Near the top, the IZ raised a massive hand, into a fist. Everyone stopped behind him, like (now broken) clockwork. The stench, the acrid synergy, with everything a crowd of the devils _could become_ was incredible but could only affect the living. The IZ could provide food—that's all the demoniacal goblins really knew.

He was working on it.

Just when the group reached the fifth floor, of a sudden, the former-corpses surprised Teresian, most thoroughly. All pushed on her and she playfully went down.

–Wow, you definitely got me! I'm done playing with you, geez y'all are fetidly brown, un-showered hobo, poopy and side-ways-stink, so up and at 'em!

Then, sinuous arms outstretched, the Wysterian raised them all up magically. But they had a plan, and death was the least of their worries. They were all in her 'magical' grip, just floating. Katrina thought it was funny, and she and the Black weapons took an initial laugh.

–Now, I think you guys should be thrown out any given window, so I think I'll—

Quickly, at least a dozen of the macabre Fretless Undead burst forth with fluid-coated vomit, aimed directly at the teeth-ridden countenance of the saurian.

There was so much of it, some of the dark juice got in her mouth.

Then, it was done.

Outraged, the saurian just sent all the Undead out the plate glass window, a massive crash, just an afterthought. The forlorn Undeads definitely opened the far window up with body-splitting power, so furious were they hurtled out of the apartment building. Then she stood up and gazed at her body.

She blinked, staring at the Black gore which was everywhere. The discharge in the Wysterian's mouth, down to her stomach, was racing along to her life-blood-stream. The Undead ichor stamped like any jack-booted thug on the innards of Teresian. Meanwhile, Teresian killed the Vast Wretchedness so there were piles of corpses, up to the ceiling. Her Black sword and all her other weapons were hard pressed, all completely un-dead-ebonized with blood, their illustrious "shiny" sheen just a memory. The floor below the roof was made completely impenetrable by the dead un-dead. The Leader astral called a retreat, but his main purpose was done. Now, with 5,000 of the Undauntables killed, he thought of that as a pin's fee, to have the dragon at his feet (or worse). On the seventh floor, the roof, he already had a plan.

Katrina was concerned when she spied the eyes of the saurian. They were steadily turning black. The childhood memories of the 'mythical dragon,' the creature that could do anything and everything, flooded back. She couldn't, wouldn't let this dragon be turned into a 'horde-monster,' no. The green and blue tint kept up a valiant struggle—they defended the twin-irises from the un-dead's vision.

How deceived the militaries were on Earth! They thought with all the power possessed by any given reptilian, that they could hurt a star dragon with weaponry. Even a neutron bomb couldn't get through that hide. They didn't even think to get the dragon sick with a mere virus. Maybe, back there, they didn't have a known-plague that could make a saurian ill. Didn't they read <u>War of the Worlds</u> by H.G. Wells? Just 'living' on Earth infected the aliens. After all, Larascena got sick. Did it come from Earth, like tuberculosis or Ebola; was all of it 'human-borne'? Didn't Larascena know magic, couldn't she have 'wished,' the illness away? Obviously, <u>that</u> didn't work, and Katrina was reminded of the god's limitations. Then, the full weight of what it means to be a companion fell on her. If she'd only known that the virus could kill a god, or make her go *ber-zeek*, she'd have taken precautions. Now, too late.

For her part, the saurian thought magic was required to deal with viruses. The Wysterian had something to talk to Kerok about (first thing when, and if, they got to *his time*).

Katrina then came up, questioning, all the Black weapons around her.

The Wysterian turned to the teen.

–I think. I'm in trouble.

The four Beachers remained were they were (Bob just arriving, taking possession of a Black knife) but they hadn't lowered their guns. Katrina didn't see the connection, at least, not right away.

–That got them out of here, great! You're okay, right, Teresa?

–No. I was too prideful, didn't think the Undead could hurt me in the least. I'm wiser now. Hindsight outweighs foresight, and I see the reason why. I had a hint this might happen. Pride allowed me to cast that forewarning aside. I wish I had that back. It wasn't your fault. No one can oppose a dragon's pride. That, unfortunately, includes you, my pre-dragon.

Katrina was depressed entirely, and she couldn't believe it, suffused with tears, leaning into Teresian's huge shoulder. The Black weapons too were aghast. They were totally taken in by the IZ's overall plan. What was laughable to them formerly became a horror show.

Conscious of the fact that the Russian teen and the Black weapons looked up to her didn't escape Teresian. She did a "toweling" off of the black blood with a sudden whisk of her sinuous-serpentine self. Then, she scrutinized the Beachers with some restored confidence. The Wysterian deftly shook it off.

—Alright, nothing has changed, my dears and my children. I'm just doing a little internal damage control, that's all. There is nothing to worry about. I'll fly us off the roof of this building. Getting us back in time will be the responsibility of the Black weapons. There are only two flights of stairs left to us. Let's go!

CHAPTER SIX

APARTMENT ROOF RISING

ROBERT FISHER WAS IN THE MANAGER'S OFFICE, AND THE OTHER three 'Beachers,' hurried to find him, accompanied by the two companions. Bob heard the fight, below, and knew that ammo would be a priority.

The manager's office would have been a total bore to the Wysterian, all it had was guns infinitum. She'd no use for such primitive things.

With the hell-fluids doing battle with her own Wysterian blood, she felt so weak that a gun might be a good choice. Her five Black weapons so disagreed, creating a sizeable dispute about who could defend a declining Wysterian. Immediately, they accused each other, none wanted responsibility for the Wysterian's being infected by demonic fluid.

The two companions, back together, spoke in a low voice.

–I think I'm in contact with the soulless leader.

–The 'head' crap-face bogey, right? Yeah, I got a glimpse of him. I'd love to deal with him if I wasn't so incredibly weak. I'd make him eat his brain, appropriately enough.

—Yes, him. He's got the blackest personality I've ever felt. I'm kinda new at this telepathy thing, though. You understand my star dragon.

—Is he intelligent?

—He's dark and smart, my eminence. That's as far as I'm going. You know what has to be done, however.

—No, I won't allow it, human.

—Normally, as your dutiful companion, I'd acquiesce, my queenly Wysterian. You are weak and need my protection. I'd die myself if The Horde conquers my star dragon. You will allow it and you will watch my victory. Because victory will be mine!

—You are well-trained, and I blame myself completely for this. I love you, Kat.

Katrina was silent, looking deep within the Wysterian's troubled eyes, the Unbeacherly-black attacking a fortress-like structure, that was her double-irises, and the defenders giving slowly in, into the depths of darkness.

—That won't save any of us, my friend. I'm sorry about that, your love should have nothing to do with your strength, but in this case it does. I've got to confront him. We don't have much time. The Black weapons need to get all of us back, well, in Time! There is no other solution that I can see.

—Thesis, antithesis, synthesis, right, Kat? Maybe I'll think of another solution to our dialectical problem?

—Dream on, saurian. I'm living in reality, and you are coming with me, even if I have to carry you. I've got that kind of implacable strength, I can easily do it, mind.

The saurian winked.

—Wow. Some kinda yikes, I've created a monster!

The vicious Un-animated focused to chomp on anything with a pulse and that at super-light speed. This told Katrina loads the impressive pace of someone close to death; or over it, into the world beyond. The Undead were the quick ones. They were hungry.

At the outset, the Black swords could manage it, but as the crowd gathered to an overwhelming (and running) size, they got worried. All the while, the Wysterian continued teaching the Black weapons, in her mental classroom, about Time Travel. She concentrated on going back in time, forward, not so much. All the Black World weapons were considered students. Now, just on lunch period, they were 'assisting,' with just a few of the Undead. Rabidly bored with the blood and gore, Teresian ordered the student's back to class.

Alright, everyone come in, right to class y'all.

Katrina's sword spoke for all, then, sort of a relief to the Black World weapons.

We are under attack from these demonic ghosts. Do we have time to learn from the master? We need some chimney relief!

Oh, this is nothing! And I'll sweep your chimney, every one of you. All of us, mentally present, school begins again!

In Teresian's mind, all the Black weapons attended class. Katrina just sat in the back, in a crappy mood. She was just auditing the class anyway and wouldn't be burdened by a grade. It was difficult, but not too difficult for a Black World Weapon (a BWW, in Brian Miller's 'shortened' genre). By the way, I *hate* the word 'genre' jes' saying.

CHAPTER SEVEN
COMPANIONS OF THE FUTURE

BOTH KATRINA AND THE SICKLY WYSTERIAN HEEDED THE GUN choices. Just now, Katrina thought of using dragon-fire to drive the masses away. Now, with the Wysterian's magical power a long memory, she regretted not thinking of such a basic thing earlier, not thinking of the concatenation of events. She was lazy in her thinking, not being a dutiful companion at all, and now the saurian had to pay for it. She got her mind off the troubling bad choices, looking at the guns. A Stakeout shotgun suited Katrina just fine.

–That's just your style, but not mine. I'm an 11-foot-tall Velociraptor (and a good-looking Velociraptor, too) and I see something just for me.

The Wysterian spied a 'big,' weapon, beyond anyone's reach. She took the thing down; it was almost 10 feet up, on three metal props. It wasn't a shotgun; it was an anti-tank rifle. Incredibly this one had several boxes of shells, just lying on a desk. All the teens just thought they were mortar rounds. This was easy packing for any given saurian, but this Wysterian had Unbeacherly blood in her. It was all she could do to lift the thing, but her nimbleness made it look like no problem. In the Wysterian's disabled condition, this was the gun for her.

Katrina took a whole slew of shotgun shells for her Stakeout. This one held eight rounds at a time, and she loaded the gun methodically.

Then David spoke to the star dragon, on seeing <u>her</u> pick.

–Hey, hey, that's not the gun for you; those shells are the biggest I've ever seen. You're as weak as a kitten. That thing weighs more than a hundred pounds! Damn, you can't lift that, in your shitty condition.

Irritated at the little mini-spaz attack, the Wysterian whirled on David, aimed the anti-tank gun right to his surprised forehead, lightning quick.

–This way I'll hit what I aim at. If we didn't need all hands, I'd decapitate you instantly, obviating your cranium to the nearest wall. Don't prove troublesome to this dragon. I'm in a mood.

–That does it, Kat. What kind of a dragon am I anyway? I'll fly you off this stupid structure, with you teens attached, we'll all go back in time with the Black weapons help and we'll save Littorian and Brian! I have said it, which makes it so almost done! You Black weapons, it's just if everything fails, I'm weak, you know. Don't deprive a Wysterian of just a little fun. This anti-tank rifle will be my <u>second</u> ass-kicker, after you guys, okay?

Katrina was stuffing her pockets full of shells. When they were full to the brim (and over it) Katrina took a .44 Magnum off the wall, the biggest handgun available. She got the loading cylinder open like an expert, checked it, yup, hollow-points, then clicked it closed.

–This will do for me, and all of Teresian's excuses apply, whatever they are, my new-friend-dies. With my Stakeout too, I'm ready. Sorry, my Black weapons, I'm just looking for some added insurance. You can spank me later, my weapons, if we make it.

Normally, the Wysterian can counter the zombie blood by magic, and this the saurian *did* try. It wasn't working. This was another frustration from the Beacher World. Teresian wasn't at all used to it. David had enough and scoffed at the anti-tank gun in the Wysterian's claws.

In high school, or the equivalent on this planet, Dave had been a wild one. He knocked out two teachers, in a rampage. The teachers had a freight train enter their surprised faces. Then, he actually spit on and struck the principle, too. In gym class, he did questionable things in the locker room. At one point, he waved his privates around like a massive lasso, Dave was hung like a giant Equus stallion. He intimidated all the boys in his class, even throughout the whole school with no problem, he was the supreme Alpha male. Dave was about to go to juvy hall, on punching out the principal, when the *Incident* happened. An Unlifeless apocalypse was the result. The virus got hold of every human, and only a handful remained immune. David addressed the Wysterian, his desperateness and his temper leaking out. All David's 'niceness' was thrown away.

CHAPTER EIGHT

Ground is Undead

David Williams decided to keep it street.

—It's like this, Miss Dragon. All the service ladders we had to throw to the ground, so Black-zombified Lurids wouldn't climb up, see? With that intelligent zombie's direction, they can climb up this building all piled up on top of each other. Someone's got to take that IZ-shit-bag out. The elevators don't work, and you can't use the balconies to fly us out of here, or whatever, those are all on the lower floors. Those infected are fast, can break down doors with one hand and chow on your guts. Soon as you die, once bitten, you become like them. You have to blow their brains out, you get that, you wily, serpentine bitch? We *could* fly off the roof, if you could manage at least that! You see the shit we're mired in?

Katrina was furious.

A bitch!

The star dragon blood in the Russian raged and her sinewy arm rose.

Teresa stepped in between them, with an *I'll handle it*, expression. The Wysterian was not herself, fighting the Black-blush-blood within her. She didn't wish David to have his face smashed in or, more likely, knocked off, slamming into the corridor wall.

–Then, pre-companion, it comes to this. I'll just have to fly all of you off the top of this building as a star dragon you'll arrive on the beach, pretty-as-I-please and the Black World weapons will bring us backward in time to save young Brian Miller and Lord Littorian! It's just so simple; it pains me to think of it further. Don't pain me my malleable and rubber-bone-breakable little human. You should have more respect for a star dragon's incalculable ego. If I was myself, you'd learn quickly.

Katrina, held back by the Wysterian's sword, added in.

–Don't be such a half-lush, downer-boy. You have to blow all their heads off, that's all. Should be pretty simple for you.

–What you're a Russian, right? You presume too much for any humanoid, that's for *shackled*. We don't all have star dragon blood racing through us. Your people must be full of pansies and lunatics, just judging from your example, you little buga bear. Back to you dragon: You've internal caked-on-zombie-blood in you. I'm down with killing you before you turn *ber-zeek*.

The Wysterian just laughed (but still…), then narrowed her eyes.

–Oh, he says such cheeky things! I can feel your fool skull crush and splat under my claws, a small accomplishment, my little David. You should see me when I'm better and, yes, run in fear. I'm colossal, enormous, Herculean, yada-yada-yada.

The saurian good-naturedly petered out, not wanting to be unctuous. Plus, spying Katrina, just there, she didn't want to have all those synonyms for the Wysterian's mightiness spoken out. She wanted to hear that from Katrina. David was nonplussed.

–You're weak, dragon. Your ego accomplished that much. You probably can't even injure a mouse right now. Your scales couldn't even stop this gun from working, if I wanted it to.

That grated rudely on the reptilian, and she gnashed her still-sizeable teeth. Katrina just sucked her <u>own</u> loudly. She'd never, ever heard a star dragon talked to in such a way. David was turned into blowing dust if Teresian just let her act on his person.

–Don't play vermin with me, master peddler, I've got a boat load of human power, don't mess with me. I'm a serpent and can tooth-you-to-death. Even if I have to reach down your throat, grip your sphincter and mightily yank, I'll win this lubricious debate.

Then, given her gargantuan size, Dave backed off.

–I overstepped your *Mad-gesty*. Can you forgive me?

–That's some improvement.

Katrina noted the 'mad' comment in his mischievous reply, but just let the whole thing go.

At that, David gingerly maneuvered under the Wysterian's left muscled arm—the muscle didn't move and either did the star dragon.

–I can't pull you forward at all! Katrina must have the strength of gods to get you going!

–*Star Dragon gods*, thank you. Feeding her the Tree of Life enstrengthened her beyond reckoning. She could take on the Un-Crimson-Horde, but I'm holding her back, by strength of will (only). I'd let her smash you, a brief affair, but we need all hands at the moment, is that okay, Kat?

Katrina's urgency to throttle David subsided. Instead, though, she had a permanent, but subdued rage against him. Never had a star dragon been talked to in such a way—except, more tamely, by Brian Miller. He was the one human Katrina exempted. The fact that the teens were off-worlders and weren't 'humans' at all didn't interest the Russian. They talked and seemed like humans, so they should have a good level of respect.

All the Unamorted that approached the Beachers and her companion got a taste of the anti-tank rifle. The veins in her arms straining to the max, the Wysterian shot the Ravaged with complete abandon. All the ghostly got holes in their heads, she hit them in no other place, her marksmanship perfect. Even the whole cranium was buzzed and severed-off on numerous occasions.

For the Russian teen's part, she fed into the Horde's collective mouths all the buckshot she had from her Stakeout. The other Beachers spent their rounds the same way, quickly exhausting their ammunition supply. Many, many heads were splattered on the walls and, yes, the ceilings of the stairs going to the roof.

The Wysterian, leading bravely at the outset, was taking up the rear, torpor and ennui replaced her native dynamism, heavily leaning on Katrina. All the while, her anti-tank rifle was doing its grim work on the Horde behind her, leaving torrents of brain-guts.

–How are you doing, my star dragon?

–I'm doing the easy ones twice, my companion. Don't <u>worry</u> about me (just <u>hold on</u> to me).

Many of her rounds found two heads, sometimes three or four, as she leaned on her companion. In her reptilian mind, she had to fight the anomalies of the blood raging in her system and get the teens down to the beach as a star dragon. As she *click, click, clicked* along, her doubts were hills, mountains, and, then the supreme <u>Everest</u> as she slowly maneuvered up the stairway. Naturally, she hid those thoughts from her companion. Soon, the doubts grew into Mount Olympus and then (even) some.

Someone else noticed the *clicks*, and then planned.

CHAPTER NINE

THE THUNDEROUS

ONE LEVEL TO GO, THEN, THE ROOF. THE IZ WOULDN'T HAVE THAT, however. The star dragon fascinated him, and he wanted to rule over the great beast. He'd risk any amount of Goo-Blacks to have her reigns in his Cyclopean hands, to control her as an Undead Horde Monster.

He figured without Katrina.

The IZ acted.

—Right there, my blackies! Now!

The blood-splattered Day-Crawlers pushed on the rickety wall supports, just plowing them over. This floor was undergoing a renovation, and the IZ took full advantage, sending the Undead beasts against it, thereby ruining the ceiling above them.

Of a huge sudden, the floor fell in, but it didn't fall like gravity had anything to do with it. It just disappeared. Many of his people were destroyed, but two of the virus-less fell too.

Instinctively, Katrina needed to make a choice. She could save her saurian companion or the Beachers. She cheated, and screamed out to them, but doubled back, and pushed the Wysterian against the far wall.

The reptilian lurched against the wallboard, denting it in. Katrina was there, comforting her, grabbing her arm, and pulling her forward, destination, the roof.

–I couldn't lose you.

–I know. Now, save them, and we'll get to the roof. I've just enough strength reserved to get us all off the top of this building. The Black weapons know all they need to know about time travel, class is quite through.

David Williams, both legs broken in the fall, wouldn't go out easily. His .45s blazing away, sent bullets through the brains of 16 Undeads that approached him. Then, he had to reload. It took him a few seconds, and 16 more were just chowder. Reloading again, 50, 100, 200 zombies were on him. Zhao Ziyi was unconscious and didn't feel her limbs under the grasp of the Outlandish. The whole Horde of them, literally went out the windows, Teresian's sword mistakenly thought they were going *down* the building, many just falling. The Black sword didn't see the Unbeacherly structure outside the building, and now that churning Armageddon was growing to the roof.

Hurrying to the hole, once her dragon was safe, Katrina was aghast. David Williams and Zhao Ziyi were chopped and eaten right before her eyes, in the time it's taken to read this sentence. All the weapons, except for the group-defending knives, went down in the hole, and fought the loathsome Nosferatuians, but they were far too late.

Bob and Nausicaa didn't even have time to raise their guns, it happened so fast. The knives attached to the remaining Beachers were trying to decide to go down the holes, to defend the fallens. They just remained with Nausicaa and Bob. The Black swords were just arriving. One winked look, they knew they were way too late.

The IZ, retreating too, had a Beacher teen prize, pulled at the last moment, and he laughed to himself.

Katrina addressed the shocked Beachers.

—Go around the rim of the hole, on the left, there.

—Don't you think that if we—

—I said let's go, come on, go, *go*!

Katrina, almost on the top floor of the apartment, was entirely carrying the Wysterian, almost limp in her mighty arms. She started to feel the strain, just slightly, but they were just one flight away.

No more Beachers are going to die, no more! Hear me, Wysterian! I wish I had five minutes with that IZ, I'd kill him!

Katrina, bitter now, headed up the stairs, and pushed the door open, breaking the heavy-set lock holding it closed. The door, which could have sustained 20 men beating for weeks on end, came off its hinges and the lock split like a matchstick.

—That door was indeed toddler's play! We've arrived, my companion, I see the sun! You can fly us down to the beach; the weapons know how to go back in time, we've crystal-clear made it!

—I can fly us down, you'll see my companion. I'll get my magic-fantastic back. I'm sorry about the other Beachers.

—I know. Just look here, if you fly us—

Katrina's stomach clenched at the sight in front of her.

The IZ was there at the far end of the building, right were Teresa would have launched her dragon-self skyward. He and all his zombies must have climbed out the windows to face them on the roof. In his mighty hand, was the head of David Williams. Shocked, one of Katrina's knives went forward, in a flash. The IZ no longer held the severed head. The knife, at ultra-speed, cast it into the shore-bound waves, and then hurried back to Katrina's side.

The IZ pointed at the knife, and did a 'NO' with his head, looking at Katrina.

The IZ was in a narrow corridor, waiting for the group to arrive. Zombies accompanied all the empty space Katrina was expecting. They stood, looking at the IZ, subdued, staring away from Katrina. The Beacher teens stopped too, scanned at each other in fright, and then gaped at the Russian. Katrina turned to them, and she smiled grimly. The teens cocked their machine gun bolts back. Katrina raised her hand to stop them from shooting. She knew it was between her and the IZ, no one should interfere. The Wysterian, supremely weak and barely holding on to 'herself,' was set to the side of the doorway, by a tender Katrina. The anti-tank rifle exhausted, the saurian threw it down. The Beachers, for their part, had only a few rounds left. The reptilian was just about to speak.

–I know what you're going to say, just don't, don't! You loved me, and I needed to be loved, I wanted that, the great Wysterian fulfilled my need and more so. You know I couldn't lose you. I love you and that's just about all I know. I can't let that IZ bozo take you, I can't. I have to do this.

–Kat, if you ever—

–I know, I know, but it had to be this way—and I've got your star dragon blood in me, I know what I'm doing. Don't interfere, you Black weapons, just stand by. If things go south for me, butcher the Undead, especially Mr. IZ, there. Do him first. At least I'll be avenged. Fly to the beach, the Black Weapons will get everyone back in time.

Katrina's sword swelled above the rest of the chiming knives, hatchets and Teresian's blade.

–You can't Katrina; he's mightier than you ever—

–I'm mightier too, don't worry; defend the group, I'm counting on you!

The Intelligent Zombie raised his index and middle finger up to his black eyes and then pointed them at his own eyes and then back at Katrina. Then he took his mongo fist and slapped it, with an incredible whoosh, into his left hand. He pointed at Katrina then, with a smile.

–I see your shit-eating grin, and I'll just raise you *my* brand of karate-dragon. You'll live to regret my kung-fu in your fool face (oh, no you won't!). I'm the *dragon now, pure dragon*, come on!

The IZ raised his Brobdingnagian hands, doing a thundering bicep bulge. Then, he raised his left hand, simulating opening up the corridor, in which he was 'confined.' The Undead miscreants dutifully tumbled over the edge of the apartment, crashing to the pavement below. Then the right hand, and again, zombies fell off the building, until he balled up his roaring fist. Even with that expenditure, there were 600 or 700 Undead crowded together, all awaiting orders. The IZ had an announcement.

–I kill!!!

Katrina scoffed and definitely sucked her teeth.

–Yeah, right, and that's "I will kill you," crap-for- Undead brains. That's all you've got to say? Too bad it's autobiographical, but I knew what you meant.

She fought like a Wysterian, and though she wasn't as powerful as the IZ, she avoided his fist strikes. For those she couldn't, Katrina successfully blocked each one thrown. Not so the gawking zombies though, and Katrina could see the results. The missed IZ punches landed like lightening and when straight through the faces of the slack-jawed on-lookers, making their countenances fissiparous. In short, the Undead craniums looked like a piece of dynamite went off when the IZ hit them. Any Lizardanian, Crocodilian or Alligatorian would be proud of the way the human teen smushed the shit out of the 10-foot-tall muscle factory. She smashed the IZ's face with so much force, right in his lower jaw that his razor-like teeth flew out like shrapnel, into the hapless Undead. Spit and blood covered at least a dozen of the On-Donut-Ers. She hit his shoulders with her forearms, breaking the cement under his feet. The teen Russian was the absolute <u>queen</u> of elbow strikes, tiger claws, ab smashes and haymakers. Katrina was indeed the <u>dragon</u> of pugilism. Her multiple (and sideways) mid-air kicks rang like a gong on a mammoth-ship bell. The IZ had never been brutalized so harshly. In one of these foot kicks, Katrina rose up into the air and had her heel crash into the IZ's face, then landed back down, gracefully. She ran full-force to the IZ, hitting away, giving him his <u>*own*</u> bloody taste of zombieism. It wasn't one of Katrina's best fights, but the girl had so much heart in each one of her punches. In truth, it was her *first fight.*

Teresian, propped up against the doorway, stared at the spectacle. She was shaking at all the hits the IZ gave Katrina, and the Wysterian <u>felt</u> them, too. All of this was one bitter irony, to the reptilian. Before, when the Twins of Triton threatened Earth, she impersonated Katrina, shape-shifted and really surprised Larascena. She could see Katrina fight. She transferred all her remaining energy into Katrina's physique, with *will* alone, but still maintained enough energy to fly the teens off this roof. That's primarily why she wasn't fighting right now. Then, Teresian grimly calculated, she'd be so done when they reached the beach. The Wysterian would have to rely on her Black World weapons to get them all back in time.

The IZ slammed Katrina in the neck with his troll fist. That got Katrina really mad, as she went backward. The group was horrified to hear a tone from her, a snarl and a wolf-like sound. It was a vicious *she-wolf* ferociously growling.

At the end of the five-minute fight, the IZ got Katrina on the ground. One bite would finish her. Only Katrina's hand, steadily weakening, was preventing him from scoring one on her handsome, but skinny, neck. Her words, previously spoken, held Teresa and the group back now. She raised her other hand to them, urging them to steady down. Then she heard a guttural sound from the ravenous, bleeding leader of the Resident Hucksters.

–Got you bitch!

–That's your first mistake. You think you've won, right? You want to take my star dragon away from me? You know why you can't fight? Because you don't stand for anything, you don't believe in anything, you are just <u>*not*</u>! Sure, I'm going to die, but not in this lifetime, and not from a stupid dummy like you. A little up-close-and-personal time is all I needed. At least you didn't call me a "c-word" and that's a credit to you, but this isn't!

At that, her long, golden hair had its turn. She swung her mane around, in a speed beyond measure, light speed, or more, and parted through the football-neck of the IZ. A torrent of blood was released, a black splash scattering over her locks, and some of it got into

Katrina's mouth. Victory was Pyrrhic; she knew some got down her throat, down to her stomach. Immediately, she felt the zombie blood and her own Wysterian blood doing internal battle.

The IZ's cranium was off, flying skyward in a zombie-seen induced arch. Still the Undead stayed black-eye motionless. The fact that their leader was no more didn't affect the Nameless at all. Still the headless leader's grip somehow stayed the same.

–You're not letting go. Just save the zombie drama for your llama. I quote <u>Nosferatu</u>: "The darkness of the death bird was blown away," and you'll get blown away now!

Katrina kicked the decapitated gunk-face square in the chest with all the strength she had in her toned left leg. It caved the chest right in, but mercifully didn't pass through. She did feel the IZ's backbone break through her Lizardanian boot.

–Oh, you know that spine snapped, hopefully you've got Obamacare, Mr. IZ-Bozo! Don't worry about my hair, it's not like someone murdered a Furbee!

Her kick sent the back-shattered cadaver 15 yards away, right into the group of vacant sludge skulls, toppling half a dozen over the edge.

Katrina knew what to do. She smiled at the Beacher movie-struck teens. Katrina was about to become the Undead too. But not yet!

All the crud-craniums moved at one time. Katrina felt the gunk blood flowing through her body. Her frame hurt mightily, due to the cement-ripping-punches of the Horde Leader. She set this aside. The Black World weapons would have to defend the group. Katrina's star dragon blood was losing to the glob-soul-busting-almightiness relentlessly flowing in her veins. Still, the Russian held her humanity, like the hero she always wanted to be. Katrina, not looking back at the group, knowing the ghouls would follow her, ran at a jog to the edge. Now completely <u>over it</u>, she started running.

Death was preferred to an Undead gook-life, trying to rip the guts out of her friends. That couldn't happen to this teen Russian.

She was happy to destroy the IZ; being killed by the cement was preferable. Her weakened, frail body, spent during the IZ fight, couldn't resist the upcoming crash. The muck-blood was running rampant, she couldn't take the 'ber-zeek' lust coursing through her, she so wanted to take a bite out of any living thing. She counted on Teresian, but it was just like playing the lottery, playing Powerball, Katrina knew her chances were grim.

Over the edge Katrina went, with fifty crud-heads right on her heels, over the edge, seven stories coming violently up. Knowing it was too late, in her weakened condition since the fight, she hoped she'd die quickly and quietly.

Her star dragon had other plans.

–Going so soon? Fortunately for you, this reptilian knew what you meant! And wasn't my flying over to get you a sprezzatura-eleganza move? Now, how is that for Universalian, huh? Now I got you back twice, my child Katrina!

Four human hands reached out in mid-air to grasp her. The Wysterian, confident the Beacher teens could catch her, wings extended out an absurd 80 feet, had all the weapons there as back-up, just in case they neglected to grasp her. One hand missed her completely, but all the others found her robe, pulling her up on the star dragon (for *star dragon* Teresian was!). Teresian managed to get one of her long legs on the cement, and then cast off with her talons biting in, repelled up. Her huge tail acted as some insurance whacking and smacking the Horde around, smashing them into miscellaneous city buildings.

The maneuver was complicated for the Wysterian, but she willed it to be so, her pennons emerging out, just like before. The only thing was, these wings weren't emerald, as usual, but solid ebony. Teresian missed the green pinions but had no time for lament. The Wysterian's wings, elongated, corded extensions, like an enormous bat on super-steroids, swooped in, the teens grabbing Katrina and pulling her up for the ride *to continue* her life. Nausicaa and Robert pulled her up between them, Katrina taking a familiar seat on Teresian's back. Muck-bloods came up and gripped onto the Wysterian's wings. The saurian swung her tail down, pasting the Undead like cockroaches, and then was airborne, quite out of their jumping reach.

–Glad you're not done with me, my Beachers. Sorry for not saving—

Bob cut Katrina short, releasing her robe.

–There was nothing you could do, Kat. All of this, this life here, will be in the far-future.

Teresian flew with a purpose and it would be her last flight in this _Time_ (she hoped). The fortress within her was slowly giving in to the Sickly-Destitutes. All the Wysterian's reserves were in the Keep, the Castle Keep, where she'd make her defense of the mind itself. What barred the last gate, the last door, was her love for her companion, for the teenager sitting atop her. The mind can be a fortress, but it is also your last bastion of absolute freedom. Give that up, permanent death, a welcome respite. The Beach Horde was strong, the heralded door weakening, their hits denting in the Australian Buloke door at every turn. The Wysterian knew all these things and it was more than mere imagination in her besieged mind. Still, her weakness continued, grinding her down. That weakness was brought on by pride, the same kind of pride that allowed the disguised Wysterian to defeat Larascena during the Twins of Triton adventure. Larascena let pride have command, and so the Wysterian learned nothing from the event. She was learning now.

As she flew toward the Beach, her black wings steadily decaying and her speed diminishing she so regretted the Undead bleeding into her mouth. The Wysterian allowed it just for fun, so impregnable did she feel at that time. The reptilian wanted that time back; it just couldn't be. The saurian sought to show-out-and-off for Katrina. Struggling along with the last of her black wings turning to wisps, Teresian knew there was only one way out of this lingering morass. The Black weapons and their ability to carry them all back in Time was her solution. They'd only have to worry about Time, she'd manage the distance, the three miles to the beach, three teens sitting atop her (and encouraging her, their voices sweet).

Yes, Teresian's mental class was complete; she'd taught the Black Weapons all she knew about time travel. They were set up in a Time Ellipse, floating in the air, every weapon devoting their mental energy to the flight back.

–It's *your* time, my brave knife, get ready to be thrown.

–I'll see you back in Time, trust to that, Nausicaa.

–It's on the beach, and I see a light shining on the very spot, can you see it, my knife?

–And on that <u>spot</u> you'll be standing.

Nausicaa and Robert saw the wings fading on the star dragon. They'd just reached the beach. As Bob focused back, he could see the Horde rushing down to the shore, in three waves. Even leaderless, the Fetid Crawls never gave up. The third wave appeared so large it must have been millions of Red-Undead, rushing down. The fading, faltering star dragon was their target, and they'd crush her completely under their stamping feet. The south and north end of the Beach couldn't be seen, it was crowded to the hilt with the Horde. The others came from the apartment building and from every street, running with inhuman (or in-Beacher) speed.

–Nausicaa, did you see—

–Yes, Bob, I know, prepare for a sandy landing!

–Hey, how much ammo you got, Nausicaa?

–I'm out, Bob.

–You might have just written our scratchy epitaph. I've already thrown my gun down; it's as empty as I feel. I hope it hit a spook in the noggin.

Just then, as they sailed past the taller structure, the Undead jumped down to tackle the Wysterian riders off, not even caring about the danger.

–Didn't see this coming, Kat! Hold on to everyone!

The Wysterian did a slow motion 360 degree turn in the air, most of the Mire-blooded had nothing to grab on to and fell to their head-smashing now-permanent-death. Katrina took her handgun, and shot through the faces of the others, attached to the dragon's dark wings. There was only one left, and he was struggling up, doll's eyes blazing. Katrina's gun was empty. With star dragon might, one-quarter of the way through Teresian's turn, she threw the Magnum at the head of the last Black Blood. The .44 cut half of the head off and he tumbled. Then, the Russian teenager stretched her long legs over the back of the Wysterian, totally enstrengthened cords, and gripped both Beachers. The Beachers sang an impromptu song as they swung around, deafening Katrina. The holophrastic phrases were Greek to the teen Russian. It wasn't a Wilhelm scream, certainly not that, but it caught Katrina off-guard.

I guess I'm used to this kind of flight, my Wysterian. I wasn't scared at all. Nice move just look at them all splintered on the ground, just kreer-splat! You're tail took out dozens of them!

Strangely, Katrina got no mental reply from the saurian, beneath her.

Katrina eyed the star dragon and shrank back. The upside-down pears, the Wysterian's orbs, were almost entirely and endlessly, black. Katrina couldn't live one more day without this dragon in her life. And she wouldn't.

–I can't do it, Kat, and that's the first time I'm telling you, and that's the first time I've said it! I *did* try, though. Now, is this *my* epitaph?

It sounded like another person talking to her, not the star dragon she knew, and loved deeply.

The twin suns were setting, and so was the star dragon. The Wysterian crashed, but tried, at the end, to be gentle on her riders, knocking herself over on her side, taking the brunt of the landing. All tumbled into the sand, the saurian wings just a distant memory. Then, the Wysterian sighed, and that really alarmed Katrina.

Her dragon was gone.

CHAPTER TEN

BLACK-WEAPON REDUX

TOGETHER WITH THE BEACHERS, KATRINA WENT FOR A RIDE IN THE sand. For their part, the Black World weapons formed an ellipse just over the ocean, preparing for Time Travel. They rotated backwards, just like the numbers on a timepiece, going counter-clockwise. They were going faster and faster, then, just a blur. Katrina minded the Beachers and waved for them to come forward. They did walk over, and then they suddenly stopped.

The Wysterian was walking over to Katrina, too, this time as the late-Intelligent Zombies' Undead Monster. Katrina drew an 'X' with her boot, telling the Beachers to stand there. The Undead were coming down three ways to the beach, and would run the teens over, so great was their speed.

Nausicaa and Bob knew this was the end. Their weapons dropped during the flight over to the beach, they were rooted on Katrina's little 'X' and they just waited, pining away. Sometimes there is nothing you can do, when you see The Horde running, wanting just and only you, their teeth gnashing, and hands raised. Bob calculated that the vanguard was traveling 40 miles an hour, the

Horde would be there in seconds. Already, they could see the caves of their black eyes, their ebony blood-covered bodies, their disheveled clothing, pell-mell sprinting over at them.

Nausicaa gripped Robert Fisher's hands and sighed deeply. They both gave up their Black knives, threw them over to the weapon-oval, and they regretted it.

–I've never been scared, Bob, not ever. I was always calm. But I'm scared now.

–Didn't like throwing that knife over to the Time Oval, huh, Nausicaa? It had to be done. We've got to depend on the Black Weapons. Katrina will save us, believe just this.

Just then, Bob saw something bobbing in the waves. He saw the head of David Williams, tumbling over like it was a victim in a crazy dryer. He drew Nausicaa too him, depriving her of this grizzly sight. Bob decided to direct Nausicaa's view to the fissiparous, giant crowd rushing down, rather than look at the vacuous, empty face of David Williams.

–There now, I'm holding your hand and you. This is as bad as it gets, but don't count on it, 'til they get here. Then, we'll be in real trouble. On the bright side, it won't last that long.

CHAPTER ELEVEN
A Light Renewed

Katrina, seeing the Beachers bestowed on the 'X' then marched over to the Wysterian, smiling. It was a forced grin, though.

–I'm not afraid.

Of a sudden, her own female sword broke formation overhead, floating rapidly down to Katrina.

–You need me here, she's gone, and you need to face that.

–I'll face nothing of the kind. She's here, she's still mine.

–You're diluted too: Love is a universal sickness.

–It's also the strongest thing we've got going, really. I've got love for you, too, my noble, divine sword, I'm sure you can see that, right? For my dragon, it's bone-deep, this love, it's a DNA-kinda thing. And you'll know about that, too, with Teresian's sword, yes? You think he's hot, and you're right! I know you've thought about romances and I encourage it.

–It hasn't gone that far yet.

–It will.

–Just let me stay with you.

–Nuh, your friends need your strength, your undivided attention. Be with them. Save us, go the the Time Oval, you hear? Save us all.

–I can defend you. Teresian's just gone, <u>gone</u>! Don't you realize, can't you <u>even</u> see, she's become one of those <u>things</u> and—

–Just get back in line, go to your friends. Go on. Now shoo. I'm with my companion, nothing will happen to me, I'll see you soon, know that!

The Black sword was sad now and just floated back to the spinning weapons.

The Wysterian, not herself at all, was full-zombie. The beast staggered over to Katrina. There was something familiar with this girl. That was all the thought that remained to the Wysterian. And the need to eat the human to drain her blood away, was consuming everything.

–I'm not afraid. Come to me, my companion, I'm right here.

Katrina stared up at the saurian Undead monster. The ocean was now a muttering, grey-chaos, mourning on the shoreline. The cloudy day got cloudier, still. They loved, but it was more propounded, more devoted, than any 'mere' love. It was universal fidelity, a sheer ultra-dependence, the quintessential part of all love, and way over it, grown to an enormous size.

Then, Katrina's legs were swept and batted out by the Wysterian's huge tail. She landed roughly in the sand. To the end, the teen Russian held strong, now lying there, casually looking up. Katrina then took her outstretched arm and put her hand on her golden hair assessing the reptilian, just lying there in the sand.

–I'm more comfortable here and thank you for that, at least the weapons got away, I hate them to see you when you're still in a mood.

Almost in answer, the Wysterian jerked her head up by the hair, and prepared with a roar to crush it into bone-splinters. Katrina knew that even with her power just a memory, the mammoth, doll-eyed creature could do it easily. She contemplated the ultra-wolf like teeth, amazed that the canines were as wide as her entire face. The Undead horde was almost at the 'X' and, despite it all, Katrina was still, <u>still</u> hopeful. The Beachers had hold of each other, just waiting for the end. The Black weapons above her couldn't be seen now, they just disappeared.

–What big teeth you have, Teresa!

Katrina was thinking about Little Red Riding Hood and could almost hear the Wysterian execrably hollering *All the better to eat you with!* No sound came from the saurian except a distasteful snarl and a deep growl.

Katrina flashed an eye at the jaw-crushing fangs and closed her eyes.

A light appeared and suddenly the wind was blowing in the opposite direction.

Nothing happened.

She was waiting for her odious end. Still, Katrina sensed nothing except the *burning rose's* scent of the breath of her erstwhile friend. It didn't anesthetize her, at least not that much, it was slightly arousing.

Katrina sluggishly, almost reluctantly, opened her eyes.

She was physically in the head of the Wysterian and cast her green eyes on either side of her. Clouds gone, the sky, cerulean. The incredible, shiny white reptilian teeth looked like the albino bars of a prison. She felt Teresian's tongue touch her lips.

–Either you're going to kiss me or eat me. In either event, it's going to be so erotic!

Time travel had been a success, but the weapons, floating down to the companion pair, where at sixes and sevens about what they saw. The Black swords just queried with their guards lightly touching Teresian's muscled shoulders.

Then, Katrina felt the wild touch of the Wysterian necking with her, feeling her tongue because it tasted good, goodest, greatest!

Kat! Kat! Thank the Heavens I didn't eat you, at least, not like this! We can save that for later, I'm so happy I could squeeze you to near-death and I just may!

Katrina gave back on the kiss, touching the body of the saurian again, pawing ruthlessly here and there. Then, through the white prison bars, still not removed yet, Katrina saw Brian Miller, Littorian, Soreidian, Kerok and a myriad of other saurians. They were on the brink of a decision.

CHAPTER TWELVE ———

An Exceptional Afterword

KEROK NODDED TO THE WYSTERIAN AND KATRINA, NOT THINKING anything was wrong. The saurian strode over. The wise Alligatorian snickered, recognizing a deep kiss on the part of the two companions. He perceived the two teens. The Alligatorian gawked with surprise at the teen girl and didn't pay any attention to Robert.

–Hey, get a Queen-sized, T-Rex room for a kiss like that! So this is my companion Katrina? Where'd you find her?

–Oh, she's from the future. The world turned zombie, (it was just a typical case, really, and it was no problem dealing with it) and Nausicaa Lee just didn't quite fit in, just couldn't get her into the zeitgeist of that time. I thought, since you needed a companion, that she could fly back with me. Is she acceptable, my lord?

–Well, she looks Asian to me, and I'm not being racist here, and I'm not going to say 'You all look alike' or some nutty thing like that. You might be as good as Brian Miller in rustling up companions, Katrina. You, Nausicaa, aren't as 'buffed up,' as some companions I've seen, but I'm not as 'buffed up' compared to the majority of saurians. If I'm acceptable to her, she is acceptable to me.

–You are accepted by me, and I pray I'll be the greatest companion ever!

Teresian, recovered from almost biting the head off Katrina (and she'd have instantly killed herself for this, just setting magic aside), and marked the Alligatorian.

–Kerok, I've a favor to ask of you.

–A favor? It's rare that I've had a word with you, my Wysterian. I welcome this, but I've a surprise for you.

–That fault is mine, my noble lord. Surprises just after my request. I know you are the wisest of your kind. I've thought a lot about this, and it's something only your magic can do for me. I'd like to have viruses; all forms of contagion wiped from me. Can you do it?

Then the Wysterian felt light-headed. It happened only for a moment.

–Your wish, granted, my powerful lady.

–You are most kind. The story I have to tell, granting me such a request, you'll have to hear over a campfire, tonight. Agreed?

–I'm looking exceptionally forward to it, now that I have a companion from you, to boot! Now for the surprise. We found your brother.

CHAPTER THIRTEEN

WINGED FLIGHT

THE WYSTERIAN BEHELD THE ALLIGATORIAN IN SHOCK. SHE WENT forward and actually picked Kerok up, off the ground, just to stare at him better.

—My what? My brother? Ages I've been searching for him, just ages, eons! Where is he?

—And, Katrina, we found your brother, too. An interesting set of choices, there, but appropriate. Now, set me down, I'm trying to impress my new companion, and this lifting me up albeit in total joy is, well, compromising.

Teresian set him down, gently.

—Now, that's better. You, the brother-less, come with me. Then, you'll be brother-full!

Just before they left to find the long (and not so long) lost brothers, Korillia came to Robert, tapping him on the shoulder. She was so stealthy in her approach, no one noticed her (except Kerok).

—You and I are met in destiny, child.

—Ye—yes, my noble lady. We are! I will be a dutiful companion to you, my great queen!

After Katrina and the Wysterian met their brothers, cheering them both, and they chatted for at least an hour.

Then, Katrina whispered something to Teresian. All of them would talk and use telepathy around a campfire that very evening, some hours away. The sun was getting low but hadn't yet hit the horizon. The companions had the time, and permanently so.

Katrina then spoke to the Wysterian.

–Hey, let's go for a ride.

The reptilian blinked.

–Your star dragon is just waiting for you, my tender Russian! Let's scandalously *star-dragon-lee* go there!

As they flew, most serenely, the Wysterian thought. Katrina, meanwhile, was strumming away with her Fender Stratocaster, all the electricity, sound accoutrements, et cetera, magically supplied by the star dragon. The song she played was from the movie *Ink*, the title was *What Happened to You?* The teen just made up lyrics to go with the song, and it was beautiful, and she amazingly sang to the dragon in Wysterian, the ancient tongue. That electrified Teresian to no end. Katrina sang to the dragon and that really relaxed them both.

Teresian gave praise to the Black World weapons. She highly needed them. After all, Marx had his Engels, Moses his Aaron. Teresian felt positively wedded to the Black weapons. Going through time would have to be considered again, but maybe the weapons themselves could handle it. All the Black weapons were celebrating on the beach, far below the flying companions now, the scene, joyous.

Next time, however, she'd have a little more help. Littorian, Lord of the Lizardanians, liked the proposition unfolding in the Wysterian's mind, too. Littorian could go back in time, with Brian, Katrina and Teresian and the purpose was noble. Each considered the idea, totally endorsed it, and then wanted to go.

The teenage girl died in Rouen, in France, May 30, 1431. The French girl was just 19—perfect age for a companion! Littorian and

Brian wanted to rebuild 'their own' Thirty Companions, but they'd largely given that up. The Lord of the Lizardanians was ready to go home, but, after hearing the idea, maybe that could wait. The Wysterian thought a companionship, influenced by Katrina and Brian was definitely possible. With a Crocodilian peace entourage speeding toward Earth, this might be just the time.

Turinian, the new Lord of the Crocodilians and his second, Terminus, regretted killing the 30 that Rachel Dreadnought and Jason Shireman presented. Of course, that was an enterprise set up by the (late) Genotdelian. Maybe a 'new companionship,' would be an honorable role for Joan of Arc.

FINAL FIN

Printed in the United States
by Baker & Taylor Publisher Services